THE WELDING QUIRT

A Western Trio

THE WELDING QUIRT

A Western Trio

MAX BRAND™

Five Star
Unity, Maine

Five Star First Edition Western Series.
Published in 2001 in conjunction with Golden West Literary
Agency.

Set in 11 pt. Plantin by Rick Gundberg.

Printed in the United States on permanent paper.

Library of Congress Cataloging-in-Publication Data

Brand, Max, 1892–1944.
   The welding quirt : a Western trio / by Max Brand.
   p. cm.
   ISBN 0-7862-2117-8 (hc : alk. paper)
   1. Western stories. I. Title.
   PS3511.A87 A6 2001c
   813'.52—dc21   00-054254

TABLE OF CONTENTS

Lazy Tom Hooks Up with Skinny

This marks the first time "Lazy Tom Hooks Up with Skinny" has appeared since its original publication in Street & Smith's *Western Story Magazine* (3/22/24). It was one of twenty-three short works written by Frederick Faust to be published in 1924. Along with these short novels, which were published almost exclusively in *Western Story Magazine*, thirteen serials also appeared that year. "Lazy Tom Hooks Up with Skinny" is a rather light-hearted tale that features a young protagonist, known only as Skinny.

I
"SKINNY"

Take them all in all, one might have traveled in many lands without seeing at one time five such men together. They were all big, and they were all young. The thick muscles of their bodies were hard with labor, and their faces bore the stamp of experience. One might see two football teams, champions of great sections, meet on the field to decide the question of national supremacy, but among the twenty-two athletes it would not be possible to select five like these. One might go through the ranks of a brigade of soldiers, and yet the like of the five would not be revealed. What made it still more remarkable was that chance alone had picked them out and chance alone had brought them together. Wandering down differing trails, their ways had crossed in this secluded place where they were "jungling up." When they met, they instantly paid each other the tribute of mutual respect. They clubbed their fund of money together and dispatched one among them to the town to buy provisions, and, when the provisions were bought, they very amicably cooked the mulligan stew and ladled it forth in enormous portions.

It was at this time that the sixth man arrived. He was not at all like the others. He was perhaps a little older. His height was only medium or a trifle above. He was made smoothly—his hands and feet were small—his voice was gentle—his blue eyes were mild. But he bought a share of the mulligan, and, when he had finished eating it, he, like the others, selected a spot among the shadows and went to sleep.

No sooner was the hollow quiet than there was a stir among the shrubbery, and a seventh figure appeared. It was a boy of perhaps twelve or thirteen years, rather small for his age, pug-nosed, bright-eyed, as quick and silent in his movements as a mouse that steals into the pantry at midnight. He went to the old, smoke-blackened wash boiler that had served the party as a common pot, and, dipping into it, he found scrapings and remnants to make himself a hearty meal. This he bolted with that marvelous expedition of wolves and small boys, whose gastronomic powers rival those of a boa constrictor. When he had finished, he looked about him to select a victim, and presently found one in the person of the stoutest man of the party who by this time lay sprawled upon his back with his huge arms cast out to the side and his mouth open, snoring loudly. From the victim's outer coat pocket projected a small, round paper tag, with small printed letters upon it and a double yellow cord attached. At sight of this, the youngster nodded with satisfaction and drew out from the pocket a small sack of tobacco.

He dipped in his fingers again for another prize, but he found none. He tried other pockets, always with remarkable speed and yet with such delicacy of touch. His search disturbed the sleeper no more than the faint wind that stirred across his face. He proceeded to snore on blissfully while the boy victimized him more and more. The next loot that was taken was a long, strong-bladed, horn-handled knife. The boy brought from his own pocket another knife almost equally large, opened the blades of both, and then weighed them and cast them into the air, catching them with considerable dexterity as they fell. Finally he seemed to decide that the balance of the weapon that he already possessed surpassed that of the one which he had contemplated "borrowing." So he closed the latter and passed it back into the side trousers pocket of the sleeper—a feat well known among thieves to be far more difficult than to draw out what the pocket contains.

What he next secured from the large sleeper was a stout leather wallet or purse containing various things such as thread, needles, a bit of wax, a few fishhooks, *et cetera*. These he dumped into one of the side pockets of the victim's coat, which were most easy of access. From his own pockets he then produced similar articles of necessity to the Bedouin life that he led and secured them within the leather purse. Last of all, from the recumbent he took a thin package of brown papers and some California sulphur matches.

After this he seemed satisfied. He retired to the side of the glade and squatted between two tall shrubs, so far back that he could not easily be seen from the hollow, while at the same time, through the narrow opening in the brush before him, he could keep an eye upon all six of the sleepers. In this place he rolled a cigarette with such familiar skill that his eyes did not once leave the survey of things about him in order to attend to the delicate process of the manufacture. He tore out a leaf of the brown papers, sifted in the tobacco, and rolled the smoke, while at the same time he studied the sleepers one by one, regarded the shrubs around him, and even lifted his eyes to a squirrel that was darting along a branch high overhead.

He lighted the match in the same dexterous fashion, paying no heed to it while he sheltered it between his horny palms until the flame spread wide and seemed to be singeing the skin. Then he touched it to the end of his cigarette and began to smoke with great enjoyment, half closing his eyes, and drawing in great breaths that he expelled slowly in thin, bluish mists. The cigarette being finished, he yawned, stretched himself, and then, retreating a little farther among the shrubs, curled himself up and was instantly asleep.

That *siesta* did not last more than ten minutes. At the end of that period he wakened as suddenly as he had fallen asleep, and stood up. He came back again to the edge of the hollow where a patch of sunlight illumined him more certainly than before. Surely there was but little flesh upon his body. The man's coat in which he was grotesquely clad hung in loosest folds. Man's trousers, too, had been cut off halfway between the knees and the ankles. And below this edge projected a pair of skinny shanks, brown-black; and brown-black, too, were the naked feet, as tough as toughest leather. His neck was so thin that one could have surrounded it with thumb and forefinger and found that the throat was well nigh as hard as the fingers that encircled it.

Viewing the sleepers again, he was obviously disgusted by their long-continued repose. To his own insect activity the slightest nap was as good as prolonged unconsciousness, and his thin lips, sneering apart, framed a silent word: *Pigs!*

While he stood there, his toes had been toying with a

quantity of pebbles that lay scattered upon the ground. At them he now glanced down, and then he scooped up two or three handfuls that he dropped into one of the coat pockets, a veritable hunting bag for its capacity. Next he scanned the trees nearby. Of these, he selected the largest, a great oak whose branches extended far over the hollow. Into the tree he climbed as nimbly as a monkey. He went lightly up the deep-furrowed bark, clinging with fingers and toes, quite contented with this precarious hold even when he was a perilous distance above the ground. One could see, now, the value of those grotesque garments in which he was clad, for their looseness gave him as much ease of muscular movement as though he had been naked.

He slid out upon a huge branch, his feet turned out on either side like the feet of a frog, and peered over the edge of the limb. Just beneath him laid the sleepers, and a grin of infinite satisfaction wreathed the features of the boy. His first pebble he poised with the greatest care. There was no doubt as to his target. Those whom we have wronged are those whom we dislike the most heartily. He selected as his prime victim the very man whose pockets he had so recently gone through. And the bull's-eye at which he directed his shot was the wide-gaping mouth.

The pebble, whipped downward with stinging force, barely missed that bull's-eye, but it did land upon the chin of the sleeper and brought him convulsively to his feet with a howl. Those around him groaned and opened their eyes.

"Who hit me?" thundered the big man, glowering. "What damn' skunk thought he was playin' a joke on Jeff Goodrich. Hey?"

"Lemme sleep," mumbled his nearest neighbor. "I dunno who's been botherin' you. But I wanna sleep. I'm damned tired." He closed his eyes and was lost in a trice. The others muttered similar requests.

Apparently satisfied that these lazy fellows could not have been guilty of any act of malice, Jeff Goodrich decided that the blow must have come from the tree above him. He scrutinized it with the greatest care, but the narrow body of his persecutor was now flattened against the bough, his arms stretched straight above his head, and he was quite invisible from beneath.

With the thought, perhaps, that it might have been a falling twig that had struck him, Jeff at length moved away to a spot a few yards off and lay down again. He rubbed his chin once or twice, muttered a drowsy curse directed at the world in general, and was presently asleep, to all appearances.

The boy now ventured a peek over the edge of the bough, but the moment he caught sight of the big fellow whose eyes were closed, he ducked back again to safety. For, although the man's eyes were closed, his lips were pressed tightly together, and the fingers of one hand were balled into a fist. Plainly Jeff was playing 'possum, intent on catching the persecutor, if it were, indeed, a human agent.

The act was father to the fact, however. In another moment, his deep-throated snore was muttering through the hollow, and now the youngster prepared to act again. He raised himself a little above the branch, poised the missile with a serious frown as though reproaching himself for his first failure, and shot it straight to its goal.

Right into the mouth of the sleeper went the little stone and brought him bounding to his feet, while the boy dropped flat on the bough again and lay there, quivering with delight. The language of big Jeff was an indescribable ecstasy. For a full minute he thundered oaths great enough to have fired the universe. He damned the world; he damned the trees that grew upon it. He damned his companions individually and collectively. And when those sleepy sufferers had protested their innocence, he happened to slip a hand into his coat pocket and jerked it forth again with a fresh yell. Three fishhooks were clinging diligently to the tips of his fingers. Dancing upon one foot, he drew the hooks out, moaning with fury and impatience at the same time.

"Stand up and fight, you thieves, you ornery, low-lived . . . !" Jeff shouted.

Here another voice answered him suddenly: "Who you callin' low-lived?"

II

"THE SIXTH MAN"

What is the finest hair-trigger compared with the nerves of a newly awakened man? Jeff glared with inexpressible fury at the fellow who had just spoken. Then Jeff bellowed: "I'm callin' you low-lived! You . . . !"

The other came off the ground like a tiger and dived at Jeff with a pile-driving fist. Alas for Jeff that, in avoiding that blow, he tripped over a sleeper behind him and then crashed down across the bodies of two more. It was like passing a hand into a hornet's nest. All three came to their knees or their feet. One grasped a gun that was knocked out of his hand. One held a knife, but was stunned with a crushing facer and sent prostrate before he could use it.

In a trice that whirlpool of activity had swept every one of the six into its vortex. They mingled in a whirl of darting fists, each capable of striking like a sledgehammer upon an anvil face. When a blow went solidly home, the recipient went down flat. But he was sure to be up again in an instant—perhaps with a lump upon his ribs, perhaps with crimson streaking down his face—and back into the fray he charged, stimulated to get revenge. They were all enemies now. They had even kicked the sixth man, the smallest fellow, to his feet, and literally dragged him into the fray.

Upon the branch above their heads the instigator of this riot sat poised upon the branch like a monkey, holding his sides, rocking back and forth in a delirium of enjoyment. Tears of delight streamed from his eyes. Gasping and choking, he brushed them away that he might the better distinguish each and every feature of the fight. His small fists were hard as the claws of a bird. One hand darted out with every home blow that was struck, while the other hand touched in mock sympathy the places where the blows had landed.

There is a tide, however, which sets in upon all battles, even the mightiest. Presently there was distinguishable one figure that was set apart, more or less, from the others. Darting in through the press, dodging heavy blows with the lightness of a bird upon the wing, dealing out punishing returns with either hand, shifty on his feet, deadly in his accuracy, mighty in his execution, upon this man the boy now centered his attention.

Strange to say, this dealer in destruction was not one among the five Goliaths. It was the sixth man, the smallest of the group! However, the exquisite harmony of hand and foot moving together, the coolness and caution with which he worked, made up for his lack of weight. The reaching, tearing hands of the others, capable of having crushed the breath out of his body with a single hug, he cleverly avoided. His own hands were never opened. They remained as closed, rock-hard fists, and, where they landed, men went down from a knock on the head or doubled up from a blow to the body. Such was his prowess that the little band swayed apart at his coming and closed with drunken staggering together in his wake.

Finally Jeff and another, having selected each other, grappled and tumbled to the earth, fighting like a pair of mauling bears. Of the others, one was already down. The fourth now charged the smallest man and received in return for his pains so terrific an uppercut that his feet left the ground and he landed upon his head.

There remained the fifth of the big fellows, alone. To him went the victor with the mincing steps of a dancer, floated away from a wildly swinging fist that seemed able to tear its way through his body, dipped in close—and, behold, the fifth man threw up his hands with a groan and dropped to his face.

Still the conqueror was not satisfied. The boy from the tree could see his whole body trembling with anger. He went now to the two who struggled on the ground. He caught Jeff, who was uppermost, by the broad shoulders and swayed him to his feet.

"You began this, you yaller-livered maverick!" snarled the small hero, and then he knocked Jeff headlong.

Jeff's companion refused to rise. He sat upon the ground and scowled up at the victor who now stood back with his red hands dropped upon his hips, surveying the others and breathing heavily through his quivering nostrils.

"A fine bit of fat beef," said this sneering champion. "A fine lot of five thick-headed bums. In my part of the country they throw gents like you out to the kids. And the kids eat 'em for breakfast. That's all!"

There arose a staggering gentleman whose clothes had been torn to shreds. "I'll show you a new trick, you hound dog!" he bellowed, and straightway he produced from a pocket the long, gleaming barrel of a Colt revolver. But he found himself looking into a pair of leveled guns, with the glittering eyes of the small man behind them.

"Drop that," said the latter quietly.

15

He was obeyed with instinctive awe.

"Now get out!" continued this destroyer of pride. "Get out, the whole bunch of you. Damn me if you ain't ruined my sleep for long enough. An' I sure need my rest. Hey . . . you . . . I'm talkin' to you, too!"

With this, one of his guns barked, and the bullet, striking among the pebbles near the head of one of the prostrate, knocked a stinging handful of them into his face. He came to his feet with a shout, and, still half dazed by the blows he had received and the guns that he now beheld leveled at him, he took to his heels, yelling, and fled through the brush. It was a panic signal for the others. A few bullets planted dexterously near their heels gave them an added nimbleness. Presently the hollow was as bare as the palm of the hand, and the victor stood alone in it.

After this he showed not the slightest elation over his triumph. He did not laugh. He did not even smile. But he went about the field of battle, picking up the spoils in the most methodical fashion. There were no fewer than three knives and three revolvers at hand. Of the three revolvers he tossed two away with grunts of disgust, after he had emptied them into a leather pouch that he produced for this purpose. The third revolver seemed more to his liking, for, after a long and critical examination of it, he whirled suddenly and fired at a rock thirty paces away.

A pointed prominence of that rock thereby disappeared, and the stranger nodded in satisfaction and put up the gun. Where he stowed it, the boy could not quite be sure. It had disappeared as the other pair of guns had disappeared—as though by an act of white magic.

Of the knives the stranger kept not a single one, but kicked them to the side of the clearing, and the boy, with greedy eyes, noted the places where each of these spoils had fallen.

But now, as though satisfied with his achievements, or perhaps fearing the return of the five when their panic should have subsided, the stranger settled his hat upon his head and strolled away from the clearing.

It was the signal for the boy. He went down the side of the tree with the same monkey-like agility that he had shown in climbing to his place of vantage. He gained the thick lower trunk. He was about to cast himself loose and drop to the ground when something pricked him sharply in the calf of his leg. He flattened instinctively against the rough bark, and, casting a frightened glance over his shoulder, he saw just beneath and behind him no other than the late victor of the battle, with an opened pocketknife in his hand.

"Well?" said the boy, scowling.

"Well," said the other, grinning. "What you goin' to do about it now?"

"Nothin'," said the youngster. "You got me cold, I guess. I got to give up."

"All right. Come on down," said the other, and stepped back to make way.

But that instant the boy twitched himself up the face of the great oak, working with desperate speed. A squirrel could not have darted faster in such a position, and he had almost gained safety. Indeed, he was sure that he was out of reach when an iron grip closed upon his right heel and he was plucked strongly from the hold that he kept upon the trunk.

He was allowed to fall as he could. Another youngster might have received a broken back from such a fall, but this native of the wilds turned cat-like while he was in the air and landed upon both feet and one hand. In the other hand—the right—was his long-bladed knife. Another fraction of a second and he could have recovered himself enough to leap at the man and drive the blade home. But before he could rise, a grip was upon his wrist, so powerfully fastened that the bones underneath the thin flesh of the boy turned to fire, and the knife fell from his hand.

"All right," said the older man, putting his foot upon the fallen weapon. "You little devil! I ought to quirt you within an inch of your life."

"You ain't goin' to," said the boy, breathing hard but speaking calmly otherwise.

"I ain't?" said the other angrily.

"Nope."

"Why not? Why ain't I? I got a lot of sticks around here that'd serve pretty handy for me."

"You ain't got the time to stay, though."

"Why ain't I?"

"Them five'll be back here pretty *pronto*. You know that, and you ain't waitin'."

"Them? They ain't men. They're hound dogs."

The boy grinned and nodded. "They got scared," he admitted, "but just because they got so scared of one gent, they'll all come back to find out what was the matter with 'em and how you done it. How *did* you do it, cap'n?"

At this the conqueror shrugged his shoulders and smiled faintly.

"What's your name?" he asked.

"Sammy," said the other, "or Joe, or Billy, or Skinny . . . most anything that comes along handy to mind is what they call me."

"Well, Skinny," said the fighter, "damn me if you ain't the out-beatin'est kid that I ever seen."

"What might your name be?"

"Me? My name is . . . er. . . ."

"Any old name'll do," said Skinny frankly.

At this the other laughed. "They've mostly called me

Lazy," he said. "You could call me Lazy Tom, if you'd want to. But where do you go from here, kid?"

III

" 'LIKE GOOD LUCK' "

They had been scanning each other with the very greatest care, and it was plain that they each looked upon the other with respect. Now Lazy Tom showed it by stepping back from the knife that he had hitherto ground down under his foot. That knife Skinny did not touch with his hand, but, reaching forward with those brown, nimble toes of his, he caught up the weapon by its horn handle and flicked it into his hand, where it was juggled idly for a moment, and then slipped into his clothes. The sharp eye of Lazy Tom had managed to note the keen edge of the steel and the length and weight of the whole implement.

"Sometimes better'n a gun," he suggested.

"Sure," Skinny said nonchalantly. "It don't make no noise."

"Let's move," said the other, and led the way through the shrubbery.

Skinny watched Lazy Tom's gait, shaking his head with much disapproval. No one would have recognized in this shuffling stride the light-footed warrior who had danced through the cluster of struggling men, dealing out destruction with either hand. When they got into the open beyond the shrubs and were walking rapidly down a draw, Skinny remarked: "Where'd you learn to walk?"

"My ma taught me, I guess," said Lazy Tom.

"She done a quick job of it, then."

"What's the matter?"

"You act like you was walkin' in stirrups."

"You're a damn' fresh kid," said Lazy Tom gloomily. "I

19

dunno but what you'll get a lickin' anyway."

"Me?" said Skinny with unutterable scorn. "Me get a lickin'? I dunno what you're talkin' about, stranger. You ain't seen the day when you could handle a gent like me!"

At this strange speech from one who had so lately been entirely in his power, Lazy Tom stopped short and cast a sidewise glance at his companion. "Is this a joke?" he asked.

"I'm talkin' facts," said Sammy. "Look here. What could you do with me?"

"Skin you alive, you sassy little rat!" Lazy Tom cried, and reached for the child.

Skinny avoided the reaching fingertips and danced away.

"You move like a cow," he said critically. "Them five must've been drunk, or any one of 'em could've ate you up."

With an exclamation, Lazy Tom leaped at his small tormentor. It was like trying to tag the wind. His hand closed upon nothingness again, and there was Skinny, standing at a little distance and almost behind him. In avoiding these rushes, Skinny had not so much as turned his back upon his pursuer, but, keeping his face toward the man, he had floated to one side or the other as though there were powerful springs in his toes.

"You're a smart kid," Lazy Tom agreed at last, stopping his exertions. "Maybe you're too damn' smart!"

"Maybe," said the boy without emotion. And as Tom began to walk on again, the youngster fell quietly in line with him, but at a safe distance.

"You started that trouble out of the tree," suggested Lazy Tom, and his face was darkened with anger as he watched the boy askance.

"Maybe," admitted Skinny with perfect carelessness.

"How'd you do it?"

"I laid out on a branch with some of these."

So saying, he took from his pocket a handful of the pebbles and began to throw them at rocks, stumps, tree trunks, anything that might serve as a target. His fleshless arm flew back and forth like a whiplash, snapping the stones easily out of his fingertips. The results were remarkable. It seemed that he could not miss.

"What made you pick out Jeff?" asked the other.

"The fathead slep' with his mouth open," the boy said with great scorn and disgust. "Didn't have no manners, that tramp, not even when he was sleepin'. I soaked him as hard as I could. Wish I'd had a brick instead of a little stone like one of these. Where you aimed at, partner?"

"Goin' south," said Lazy Tom.

"Río Grande?"

"Down that way, pretty near."

"Well," said the boy, "they're keepin' a mighty close watch along by the river these here days."

"Eh?" Tom said, startled.

"They're keepin' a mighty close watch. Dog-gone me if they didn't catch a couple of gents that was tryin' to break across to the far side of the river about a week back. We heard the news up here right *pronto*. Because they come from this way. They'd been doin' a little rustlin'. Nothin' enough to speak of, but they got grabbed for it. Seems like it's always that way where a gent turns around and runs. It's a pile better to stand fast and laugh at 'em when they say that they got something on you."

"Is that your scheme?" Lazy Tom asked with interest.

"Sure."

"What makes you think that I'm interested in gettin' across the river?"

"Looks to me like I'd answered enough questions," said this most assured and insolent youth. "But I'd say that if a

21

gent wanted to lie low and take things easy for a while till folks sort of forgot him, and the things that he might have done . . . or been accused of. . . ."

"I understand," said Tom, nodding.

"Well, if I was one of them gents, I'd just lay back right here in this county."

"Why?"

"I'll tell you why. There ain't been a gun play around these parts for nigh onto three years. Everybody's settin' back peaceful and not thinkin' of no trouble. They been makin' just enough money to keep 'em poor . . . all except old man Hampstead, of course. He's got so much land and so many cows that he can't help bein' like a mint, you might say."

"You know the lay of things around these parts pretty good, I guess?"

"I ain't spent much of my time around here," said the boy. "Things is too quiet around these parts to suit me none. I like a mite of action, d'you see? There ain't none around here. They got a sheriff that's been sick for a year. They don't need no sheriff, things is that sleepy. You bein' a lazy man, maybe you'd like to stay a while."

The other remained thoughtful for a time. "Is there work?" he asked.

"Sure. Up to Hampstead's place they's always work. He's always got a need of men."

"How come?"

"Well, he pays just a mite under what other folks pay, and he works the boys harder, the way that I make it out. They keep comin', and they keep goin'."

"If he pays low wages, how does he manage to keep anyone?"

"I'll tell you how it is. He won't take no man that ain't a fine rider. He's a hell-roarin' fine rider himself, is old Hampstead. When a man comes for a job, Hampstead gives him a hellcat of a bronc' to ride. If he don't look good in the saddle an' out of it, he don't get the job. So the boys keep comin' in an' tryin' out for the fun of it. A gent that has rode for Hampstead can easy get work almost any place on the range. That's the way the old man works it. Are you much with a horse?"

"Oh, I ride," Lazy Tom said nonchalantly, but Skinny, observing a certain glitter in the eyes of his companion, knew that this was a great understatement, indeed.

"Where are you bound for?" asked Lazy Tom.

"Me? No place in particular, just so long as I keep goin'."

"Who's your pa, kid?"

"Never had one," said Skinny.

"How'd you get born, then?" asked Tom, grinning.

"I dunno that I ever inquired particular into them things. I just happened along . . . like good luck," said Skinny, and chuckled at the thought.

"How was you raised, Skinny?"

"Furthest back I can remember, I was doin' chores here and there."

"When you was just a mite of a lad?"

"I wasn't never too small to lead a derrick hoss or sit in a saddle."

"Was you born that way, maybe? Just settin' in a saddle?"

"I dunno. Maybe."

"Why ain't you got a hoss with you now?"

"I'll tell you. The last one I had, I was up Montana way last winter, and we both got caught in a blizzard, a reg'lar snorter, I'll tell a man. Me and the hoss fought it out for a long time. Dog-gone me if the hoss didn't die, though. I just got through myself."

Here Tom looked askance at this cheerful adventurer. He

was as blithe as though he were telling the most common-place occurrences.

"Me and that hoss had done a lot of travelin' together," said Skinny. "Since he kicked out, I been ridin' the rods."

"Where you been on the rods, kid?"

"New York, Montreal, Chi, New Orleans, Saint Louis . . . dog-gone every place that's worth goin' to."

"What did you do for chuck?"

"I battered doors, and most usually I got some sort of a hand-out. Mostly the womenfolk wanted to take me in and adopt me, or something. Three times they got me inside and locked up in a room and put to bed inside of fine, clean sheets. But each time, I managed to climb through the window and climb down and get out. I ain't particular set on bein' anybody's son by nacher or by adopting."

"What d'you aim to make out of yourself?" asked Tom.

"I ain't got no aim," the boy said calmly.

"Well," said Lazy Tom at last, "you come on with me, and we'll see what chance I got at Hampstead's."

IV

"LISTENIN' IN"

It was late afternoon of the next day when they came into Gunther Valley. In the heart of the hollow the muddy little stream, choked and deadened by the thick load of detritus that it carried, curved back and forth in leisurely fashion with a scattering growth of willows along the banks.

Here and there were hardy range cattle that had come great distances to drink their fill and then rest for a time before starting back toward the more distant ranges where the grass had not been eaten down so closely. Some clusters were lying down. Some were wandering away in leisurely fashion.

Even while Tom and Skinny looked, they saw a number of cows come over the opposite hills at a sharp trot that broke into a gallop when they saw the water. They rushed into it shoulder deep and then drank and drank as though they were on the verge of perishing from thirst. They had been away two, perhaps three days, without drink, wandering in a distant part of the range, and, having filled their stomachs with water, they would depart again. Even camels could hardly have shown greater adaptability to desert conditions.

"Are we nearin' the Hampstead place?" asked Tom.

"Look up yonder," said the boy, and pointed.

Tom saw a cluster of pointed roofs breaking above a hilltop, and, as they climbed higher, the whole place came into view—the usual bleak-faced ranch house, the tumbling sheds, the tangle of corrals around it. Beauty has no place on a cow range, and the only true roof above the head of a 'puncher is in the thin blue sky by day and by night.

"But," said Tom, "what'll they think of a 'puncher that comes in on foot . . . and damned sore feet . . . without no hoss?"

"Hampstead don't ask any questions," said the boy. "He takes a man the way he finds him."

"He's rich, you said?"

"Him? He owns pretty near everything as far as you can see. All except down yonder."

He pointed down into a dip among the hills, into which they were now descending, while the ground, rolling up before them, shut out the view of the distant ranch house of the cattle king. Lazy Tom saw before him a squat-sided little shack staggering to one side, as though the pressure of the seasonal storms had swayed it in this fashion. It looked as though it might collapse at any time like a house of cards.

There was a diminutive old shack nearby, around which

some score of cattle were milling, restless and hungry, striving to get at the food from which they were held back by thick, barbed-wire fences.

"That old gent who owns that place, he squatted there a long time back," said the boy. "Old man Hampstead has been tryin' to buy him out. He's got all the other land here, around the valley. But he can't get Josh to move. Old Josh Peters, he won't sell and he won't move. He wants that there house and he don't want none other."

"It don't look like much," suggested Tom.

"It ain't no more'n it looks. But Josh, he's used to it, you see?"

"Is that Josh now?"

A horseman was cantering down the hillside toward the house.

"Nope. By jiminy, that looks to me like old man Hampstead."

The horseman disappeared on the farther side of the shack, and Tom and the boy, hurrying, came up to the little shack in time to hear a noisy altercation take place between the visitor and the owner of the place. They could not very well walk in at such a moment. They stayed where they were, hearing every word clearly enough.

The front door banged.

"Hello, Josh," said the voice, apparently, of Hampstead. "I'm glad to see you."

"Hampstead," the other replied, solemnly indignant, "I can't say the same back to you. Damn me if I don't wish that I'd *never* seen you!"

"Here, here!" broke in Hampstead. "That's a bit too much for you to say and for me to listen to. Confound you, Josh, you won't listen to reason!"

"Is it reason to steal my cows, Hampstead?"

"I'm sorry that your cows have been stolen, Josh. You know that I have no hand in it."

"That ain't what I know, Hampstead."

"What?"

"I mean it. Here I stand to tell the whole world about it. It happens too damned pat. You want me to sell out. I say that I won't take no money for my home. And then, damned me, if my cows don't begin to disappear. I ask you, Hampstead, don't it look like the rustlers must be workin' out of your place that lies all around my patch of ground? And if they's rustlers on your place, ain't it mighty handy for you that they should begin to pester me just when you want to bust me so's to make me sell?"

"Josh, it isn't possible that you accuse me of stealing cows?"

"I accuse men that you've give the wink to. They know that you won't bother 'em none while they're workin'. Ain't that the same as hirin' them to get to work on me?"

"I can't turn my 'punchers into police to take care of your cows."

"Sure you can't. But you can turn 'em crooked to do the stealin'. That's easy!"

"I'm glad that I have an established position in this part of the country, my friend. No one will put any stock in such accusations."

"D'you think so? Then lemme tell you, Hampstead, that you dunno what folks think about you. Pull the wool out of your ears and wake up. I'll tell you plain and simple that you've made too much money too easy and fast for most people to think that you've been honest all the way through."

"If you were a younger man . . . !" roared Hampstead furiously.

The cold voice of the old man cut in: "Don't you go pityin'

27

me because my hair's white. I ain't so old but what I can't take care of myself. I'll never be too old to handle . . . a damn' skunk!" He drew out the insult deliberately and, so to speak, cast it in the face of the other.

There was a muttered exclamation from Hampstead, but then he forced himself to become amiable again. "Your temper has been tried, Josh," he said. "I don't blame you for being angry. And you're too old and too honest a man for me to pick a quarrel with you . . . no matter how much you may want it."

Old Josh growled like an angry dog, but almost at once he spoke with a changed voice: "Anyway, there ain't nothin' gained by callin' names. I'm sorry if I've called you names, Hampstead."

"I hear no malice . . . I hear no malice," said the other smoothly. "I realize that you have had great provocation, my old friend. In the meantime, I've come over here again to see if you won't listen to reason."

"Lemme hear what you call reason, Hampstead."

"I've come here to offer you a fair price for your land."

"Hellfire," broke out Josh again, "ain't you got enough land? D'you want to rule the world? D'you have to own everything?"

"Be calm, man," said Hampstead. "We can't talk if you intend to fly into a passion every moment."

"I'm tryin' hard to be calm," answered Josh. "But damned my hide if you don't rile me, Hampstead. You got more thousands of acres than you can hardly count, and still you want more and more!"

"You're unreasonable, Josh. I've explained it to you a hundred times, and I'll explain it to you again. It isn't the number of your acres that matters to me. It's the position of them. I have plenty of range, but your land lies in a bad place for me. Every time we move cattle we have to move them *around* your ranch. Your place used to be next to mine. That was quite all right. But now it lies *inside* of mine, and that's a different matter. It's as though a family of strangers was living in a room in my own house. Privacy is destroyed. But to leave metaphors and get down to the facts . . . every day that your ranch remains in your hands it is something for me and for my 'punchers to stumble over. Our cattle drift against your barbed wire fences in the winter. In the summer they have to make long detours around the same fences. You block me from half of my ranch. Now, Josh, admit that I have a good reason for wishing to buy this land. I *have* to buy it. And I'm not trying to drive you to a hard bargain. I'm willing to pay the market value of this land, or even a little more. If you won't trust the price that I set on it, I've come today to say that I'll allow you to select a board of arbiters. We'll allow them to pass a judgment upon the value of the place, and, at whatever figure they name, I'll buy. What could be fairer than that?"

"And the stock?"

"I'll buy all your cattle, too, at a top figure."

"And what about the cows that've been rustled off of my place since I told you no money could buy me out?"

"In the name of heaven, Josh, do you think that I'd pay for what has been stolen from you?"

"Who stole it?"

"Ask those who know. How can *I* tell?"

"You could tell damned easy if you wanted to. If you was to come over here and say that you'd pay for everything just the way it stood when you made your first offer, maybe I'd listen to you and maybe I wouldn't. Damned if I don't think that I wouldn't. They's been dirty work goin' on, Hampstead. And I think that you been behind it all. I'm going to sit tight

29

an' wait an' see what happens."

"Josh," said the other man not unkindly, "you're unreasonable. You'll face starvation if you keep on in that attitude. In the meantime, you don't dare to let your cows range. They'll die of famine as soon as the last of that haystack is eaten. And if they range, the rustlers, whoever they may be, steal them."

"That's it," said Josh in a voice of iron. "You got me ag'in' a wall, Hampstead. But I tell you that I ain't beat till I'm dead, and I ain't dead yet. Go on back and tell your rustlers to grab the rest of my cows if they can. An' tell 'em that I'm as steady with a rifle right now as I ever was when I was a kid. You go home an' tell 'em that!"

"Josh, I hate to have you talk like this to me. I want you to let me repeat what. . . ."

"I don't want to hear no more, partner," said Josh. "We ain't goin' to talk no more about it. How's Sarah?"

"She's well, Josh."

"She ain't rode over to see me lately. Have you told her not to come?"

"Josh, I thought that you might not care to see any of my family . . . not even my daughter."

"The devil, man," said Josh earnestly. "That girl is a damn' sight more to me . . . than she is to you."

"You've made up your mind that I can't persuade you?"

"Listen to me, Hampstead. I got this here bit of land when I was pretty young. I've hung onto it ever since. I brought home my wife to this here house . . . which it ain't much of a house. I buried my wife from this house, and I raised my boy right here. Him and me had things hummin' and mighty prosperous when he died. Well, sir, you might say that I'm left alone, but I ain't really alone as long as I got this house that they lived in, and the chairs that they sat in, and the books that they read, and the windows that they looked out of, and the hills that they seen and walked over and called home. You can put that down inside of your head, Hampstead. I'm too old to put value on money. I'm a mighty old man, and, when you talk about buyin' my place, you talk about what I have left of my wife and my son Roger. You wouldn't've tried to buy 'em livin'. Then why d'you keep on tryin' to buy 'em while they're dead?"

"There's no use, then," Hampstead said finally with a sigh. "I'm very sorry, Josh. So long!"

They heard the departing beat of the hoofs of his horse as it went off at a swinging gallop. Presently it came in sight in the distance, a glorious red bay, shining with sweat and sunshine, racing up the easy slope that lay opposite. The rancher sat the saddle with the most perfect horsemanship, erect, graceful, yet he made a solid figure as well. He reminded Tom of a picture of some cavalry commander leading a charge, some gallant and spirited warrior.

In the midst of this thought, a dry, harsh voice said just before him: "Hello, strangers. Been listenin' in?"

V

"TRUSTIN' 'EM"

What Tom saw was a tall, lank man whose sombrero was still on the back of his head where it had been pushed, doubtless, in order that he might more easily look up to the man on horseback with whom he had just finished speaking. So there was left unshadowed a long, thin-featured face, a high, narrow forehead with thin silver hair straggling down the sides of it, a wide, thin-lipped mouth, and eyes overcast with shaggy brows. He was dressed most humbly, in rough boots, and the well-worn butt of a revolver protruded from the holster at his hip. He scowled upon them both, at first, but then his face lighted.

"Hello, sonny," he said. "You back here ag'in? And is this a friend of yours?"

"I dunno," said Skinny. "I hope so, but I just picked him up."

"Where you goin' with the kid?" asked Josh Peters of Tom.

"Ask him where he's goin' with me," said Lazy Tom, grinning. "That'd be more like it."

At that, old Josh smiled and nodded likewise. "He seems to have a way of doin' things," he declared. "What might you be aimin' at in these parts, stranger?"

"At a job," Tom answered. "The kid has been tellin' me that Hampstead always was wantin' 'punchers. I thought I might drop around his way."

"Aye," said the old man gloomily. "There ain't nothin' that he can't use some place. He's got a use for everythin' livin' . . . or dead! You're goin' to work for him, stranger? You sure that you ain't been hired by him a'ready?"

The insult in this speech was passed over by Tom, for, looking straight into the eye of the stern old man, he replied: "I come here on the way to the Hampstead place. But somehow things right around these parts look pretty good to me. I dunno know but what you might need a hand, Peters?"

At this, the tall man stared, and there was a yell of pleasure from the boy, Skinny.

"By jiminy," he crowed, "I knowed that's what'd happen!"

"You knowed what?" growled out Peters. "You talk too damn' much, kid. Why, I ain't got work enough for myself on this here place," he added to Tom. "What'd I be doin' with a man workin' for me?"

"Why, I dunno," Tom said carelessly. "Me and Skinny

didn't want to butt in on your talk with Hampstead. So we stood here and listened in on some of it. Seemed like to me that, while you was fightin' them rustlers, you were playin' a game that you was sure to lose. Because if you want to keep them cows of yours, you got to have 'em near to your house, where you can watch 'em all the time. You don't dare to let 'em go loose on the range."

"That's right, young man. What about it?"

"If you was to ride herd in the day, say, and me in the night, maybe them rustlers wouldn't bother the cows none?"

At this the other stared at him, and there was another excited shout from the boy.

"Shut up, kid," Peters snapped at Skinny. "Well, son," he added more warmly to Tom, "I see as how you're a game young gent. But it ain't goin' to do me no good. I got forty-five dollars in the bank. You mind tellin' me what I should be doin', hirin' 'punchers like any damned rich man?"

At this Tom shrugged his shoulders impatiently. "Look here," he said, "d'you aim to be right sure that Hampstead is lettin' his men run off with your cows?"

"I dunno that I'd talk so free and large about it as all that," replied Josh Peters. "But what I do aim to believe is that Hampstead has passed the wink to some crooks that, if they wanted to bunk up in his hills some place, they could work the cows on my ranch and he wouldn't have his 'punchers bother 'em none or ask no questions."

"Ah!" said Tom. "Is that the way of it?"

"Don't it look like that to you? He comes over here, and he says that he wants to buy me out and that he's *got* to buy me out. Well, he don't get no satisfaction out of me. I ain't goin' to sell, and I tell him so. He rides off, sayin' that I'm a fool. And right after that I begin to lose my cows pretty frequent. What would you say that looked like, son?"

"It looks bad, and damn' bad," replied Tom. "You might say that was the sort of talk that had ought to convince a jury, but that a judge wouldn't let inside of the courtroom."

"You know somethin' about law courts, young man?"

Here Tom flushed a little and showed his teeth as he smiled. "I know a bit about 'em," he declared. "There ain't no worse medicine than a lawyer. I know that much. But speakin' about the money. . . ."

"Speakin' about the money, there ain't none," said the other calmly. "I guess that ends the idea right off the bat, young feller."

"Maybe. Maybe not."

"What you mean?"

"Suppose that you was to hire me for the fun of the game, Peters? What d'you say to that? I've done a lot worse things in the way of amusin' myself."

Josh Peters rubbed his bony hand slowly across the tip of his nose, all the while regarding his companion with the most serious gravity. But at length a smile dawned upon his lips and spread slowly across his face. It assumed huge proportions. It wrinkled his hollow cheeks. It brought the bush down over his eyes until they were two sparks of fire behind a shadow. Then he put forth his hand and closed it over the hand of Tom.

"It seems to me like I was gettin' young, all at once, and the whole damn' world along with me. Old son, that was the way that real men used to talk when I was a kid. I ain't goin' to ask if you mean what you say."

"You don't have to," Tom replied.

"And I don't have to ask if you could take care of yourself if a time of trouble was to come along. . . ."

"You don't have to," piped up Skinny. "Why, mister, that was why I brought him all the ways along with me!"

"Hey!" Tom yelled, wheeling upon the youngster. "Did you have this here thing in mind all the time?"

"Sure," exploded Skinny, dancing out of range of Tom's clutching hand.

"All that talk about danger on the Río Grande. . . ."

"Was the bunk," announced Skinny. "They're all asleep down that way, the same as ever."

"And that chatter about workin' for old man Hampstead?"

"That was to get you up this way."

"So's I'd see Peters?"

"Sure!"

Tom leaped at Skinny. It was like rushing at a dancing shadow. So, grinning broadly, he turned back to his new employer.

"Chief," he said, "that kid has sure got a bad start in life and is bound to wind up wrong."

With a grin of still more magnificent proportions, the old man retorted: "They ain't hardly no good in him. All that he can do is to go out fishin' and catch . . . men!" He laughed uproariously at his own jest, after the fashion of those who have fallen into declining years. Then he led the way into the house.

It was not nearly so dilapidated in appearance as the outside of the shack might have indicated. It was not the dusty, unordered junk pile of the average old bachelor in the West and particularly on the range where neatness is not. Josh Peters had arranged his household with the most scrupulous care. The faded curtains on the windows, even, had been newly washed, and, although they were sadly wrinkled, they were clean. The well-hollowed floor of the kitchen over which they now passed had been scrubbed not only to cleanness, but to whiteness. The very stove was newly blacked. And the pans that were ranged along the wall shone again, with burnished bottoms. The kindling and the cordwood for the next day's consumption were piled neatly to one side of the stove.

Beyond the kitchen they reached a living room in which were united, as well as could be expected, the formal dignity and dreariness of a New England parlor and the cheerfulness of a dining hall. To one side opened the door of the bedroom, and Tom caught a glimpse of an oval-framed photograph of a stern-faced woman, a chair of wicker cushioned with faded chintz, and two tall, mahogany bedposts. There was a narrow staircase that led out of the dining room into the attic.

Altogether, it was exactly such a house as one could never imagine coming out of the brain of big Josh Peters. Another person had planned it in all its details. So much was plain. And beyond question it had come from the brain of yonder weary woman on the wall, with the foolish little bonnet perched on the top of her head and tied beneath her chin with great ribbon bows.

One could not help looking upon Josh with greater tenderness and even with a new respect, also, after understanding what manner of wife he had brought out here to the mountain desert. As for his son, his picture hung in the center of the wall on the blank side of the dining room, and one saw a duplicate of Josh himself in the lank features and the good-natured, self-conscious smile.

"Sit down," said Josh wearily, and slumped himself into a chair that creaked bitterly at the weight imposed.

Skinny was trailing in from the kitchen with a suspicious bulge and a white point in the middle of his cheek. He sat down, too, in rather a stilted fashion, and although he managed with the greatest skill to speak around the strange obstruction that was in his mouth, yet he could not conceal a certain new corpulence of which he could boast. Old Josh rose as though to walk to the window, but on the way to it one of his great, bony hands shot out and fastened on the shoulder of the boy. That narrow youth wriggled like an eel, or like a snake that wraps itself around the arm that seizes it. But the grip of Josh was iron. He compressed it, and his hard fingertips crushed their way with bruising force into Skinny's meager flesh. The latter shuddered, gasped with the pain of it, and then raised a pale, indifferent face to his tormentor.

"What was you doin' in that kitchen?" asked the old man fiercely.

"Nothin'," replied Skinny.

"You lyin' to me?" asked old Josh.

"Nope. Honest, Mister Peters, I'm tellin' you the truth."

The other long arm of Peters shot forth, entered one of the pockets of that voluminous coat in which Skinny was wrapped rather than dressed, and came forth again bearing with it a great chunk of cured ham, red with its smoking.

"What's that?" asked Josh.

"I dunno," Skinny responded with perfect innocence. "Maybe that dog-gone piece of ham might've tumbled into my pocket while I was passin'. And. . . ."

"Maybe it did," said Josh. "Maybe this here damn' can of marmalade walked right off the shelf and hopped into your pocket. Well, sir, things got the out-beatin'est way with you, Skinny. They just won't leave you alone, eh?"

And he confronted the troubled eyes of Skinny with the marmalade. Nor was that all. There was a corner of roast beef. There was a quantity of pone, and even some cold potatoes.

The marvel to Tom was that so many things could even have been located—not a one of them was visible to him as he passed through the kitchen. Yet the boy had not only smelled them forth, as it were, but he had been able to open the doors of the cupboards as he passed, extract the contents of the pans and dishes with lightning touch, and then stow them in his pockets, close the doors, and pass on, arriving not so long after the others in the front room. Had it not been for the irresistible impulse to put something into his mouth, perhaps he might have escaped with all his loot, but that had been the clue that Peters had worked.

"How'd he manage to do it?" Tom asked Peters.

"Them that want to do wrong," said the old man, "the devil puts the means of it into their heads, damn 'em. Well, son, what'm I goin' to do with you?"

"Gimme a devil of a hard lickin'," said the beaten youth, watching the face of the big man carefully.

A strange smile touched the wide mouth of Peters. He released the boy without a word, picked up the plundered articles of food, and carried them into the kitchen. Then he called Skinny.

"Sit down here, son," Tom was astonished to hear him say, "if you can eat all of this here truck, eat it, an' welcome. I ain't never yet turned nobody away hungry, and I don't figure on beginnin' no bad habits now. Eat all you can. Here's some milk. I ain't one of them hard-boiled cowmen that won't have no milk cows on the place. Here's some milk. Here's some strawberry jam, too, that you plumb missed. When I was a kid your age, I could've smelled strawberry jam a mile away. I'm sort of ashamed of you, Skinny. You'd oughtn't to've missed this. Here's some fresh bread. That was a mighty stale loaf that you cottoned onto. And if you ain't got enough in here to fill you up, jest holler for me. I got some more things downstairs."

With that, he closed the door into the kitchen and came back into the dining room to his older guest.

"By the same token," Peters addressed Tom, "maybe

you're bustin' to have somethin' to eat, too."

"I ain't. Why, we had a good meal not more'n four hours back along the road. I dunno where Skinny puts the stuff away. He's got a stomach like a snake's."

"Sure," agreed old Josh. "You take a kid like that and he can eat his own weight about twice a day. If they'd turned me loose on a whole roasted ox, when I was Skinny's age, I'd've started at one end and et straight on through to the other end even if it took me a week. That's the way Skinny is. When I get back out there in the kitchen, there ain't goin' to be nothin' left but a lump in his stomach. Damn' queer thing where things can be packed away in a stomach, ain't it?"

"Why'd you let the kid off?" asked Tom.

"Why not?"

"Ain't that one way of teachin' him to steal?"

"He was born knowin' how to steal. He can palm a card nacheral as a duck swims, though his hand ain't hardly as broad as the card he's palmin'. I ain't seen him more'n once before this, but I seen enough. He was made light-fingered by nacher."

"You've seen him only once?" Tom cried, amazed. "Why, he seems to know everything about you."

"Sure he does. Put a blotter near ink and it gets black, don't it? Put Skinny near news and he's sure to get hold of it. But lemme tell you something, young man. It's somethin' that you can use, maybe, later on."

"Glad to hear it, Peters."

"They's only one way to treat an' to handle them that ain't trustworthy, an' that's to trust 'em."

Tom chuckled.

"Now, sir," Josh said, slapping his hands on his knees and leaning forward to look straight into the face of Lazy Tom, as the latter preferred to call himself, "tell me how come you're peramb'latin' the country like this with a kid, an' how come you'll work for nothin' . . . for me? Is they somethin' up your sleeve?"

"I'm out of work. I'm out of luck," Tom answered simply. "Besides, I need some fun. That's as much as you need to know."

"More," said Josh. "Let's go out and see how much of them vittles Skinny has got outside of."

They went stealthily to the kitchen door and pushed it open.

When they looked in, they found Skinny before an untouched mass of food, sitting with his chin buried in his hand and looking wistfully through the window and far away.

VI

"A HORSEMAN BRINGS A MESSAGE"

That evening the cows, already loosed from the corrals, were wandering hastily toward the more distant parts of the little ranch, and Tom had the saddle on the horse he had chosen. It was the best of a bad lot, for old Josh, having lost the fire of youth, was by no means inclined to trust his brittle bones to a headstrong, high-stepping mustang in which speed and deviltry had equal parts.

All his horses were old familiars, therefore, dull-eyed, down-headed. Tom had looked them over with the despair of one to whom a good ride should mean a good battle. There was a second horse saddled, the stirrups being shortened to a ridiculous extent. It was for Skinny, who insisted that he would keep the night watch with his friend.

"Besides," Skinny said, "a growed-up gent don't see nothin'! They ain't got no eyes. They're always lookin' inside of themselves."

Before they could start, a buckboard drawn by a neat team of creams whirled over the top of the hill, swept down into the hollow, and drew up before the house. They were driven by an old Negro, and from the seat beside him there dismounted a pale, pretty girl who took a great basket from the rear of the wagon and with it approached the door of the house.

Old Josh came out at the same time and met her. "Sarah!" he cried.

"Uncle Josh!" cried the girl.

"It's Hampstead's girl," Skinny said to Tom. "Ain't she a looker and a half?"

"And a half," murmured Tom.

"Dear old Uncle Josh," went on the girl, "I've been away from you for more than an age, but I've thought about you every day. D'you believe me?"

"Honey," Uncle Josh answered, "they ain't no way that you could say nothin' that you didn't mean. God bless you! Lemme introduce Tom. He's helpin' me out in the pinch."

So Tom approached, hat in hand, a little red, walking stiffly, and wearing that foolish grin with which most young men come near a pretty girl.

"Miss Hampstead . . . this here is Tom . . . Jones."

"Howdy," said Tom. "Mighty glad to see you, Miss Hampstead."

"I'm glad to see you, too," she said, and she let her hand linger in his, while, searching his face, she added: "And are you really staying here to help Uncle Josh?"

"Him and me's gone partners," declared Uncle Josh. "I didn't have no coin to pay him wages. But he's takin' a chance on the future. That's courage, ain't it, Sarah? Bettin' on an old gent like me?"

"It's mighty fine," said the girl heartily.

And what a smile she gave Tom. It brought the color

flooding to his face. It brought into his heart a violent wish to utter a disclaimer of all virtues in the matter. He was tongue-tied when, of all times, he most wished to be eloquent.

She turned back to Josh. "I've brought you over a roast chicken and some other things, Uncle Josh," she said. "And . . . what's the matter?"

For the face of Josh Peters had wrinkled with pain.

"Honey," he said, "it's certainly dog-gone hard for me to say what I got inside of my head and have to say."

"In heaven's name, what's wrong?"

"Maybe it's me that's wrong," said the old man sadly. "I dunno. But . . . does your pa know that you come here with them things?"

"No, but. . . ."

"Then they ain't no use. I can't take 'em. I couldn't take 'em, anyways."

"Uncle Josh!"

"I can't, honey. Dog-gone me if it ain't hard to say no to you, but I got to do it."

She stood back from him, amazed, hurt, saddened. "Are you angry with me, Uncle Josh?"

"Not a mite!"

"Then . . . ?"

"Your pa and me . . . we're havin' trouble."

"I know. And I'm so sorry. But what has that to do with me?"

"These here things come out of his kitchen. He paid for that there chicken, and the cook that cooked it. . . ."

"He didn't! I cooked it with my own hands."

The old rancher winced.

But still he shook his head, saying: "You see, when I fight a gent, I aim always to fight him fair and square. Would it be fair and square if I fought him with one hand and let his own daughter give things into my other hand? Nope. He aims to break me. If he can, let him do it. I ain't going to get no help from his own family to work ag'in' him. Me and Tom, here, is going to fight it out with him straight from the shoulder."

"I don't understand," she cried. "I don't see why there should be any trouble. And if. . . ."

"Look yonder," Josh said suddenly, pointing up the hill. "Ain't that young Jack Talbot, that's got so sweet on you lately, Sarah?"

She flushed a little at this, and, looking back up the hill, she nodded. "That's Jack."

Tom, anxiously glancing in the same direction, saw a handsome youth careening down the hillside on a fine black horse—a veritable racer in his lines, but not more aristocratic than the face and the bearing of Jack Talbot.

"You mark what I say," Josh was adding, "he's come from your pa to tell you that you got to go on home with him."

"He wouldn't dare," answered Sarah. "He wouldn't dare to bring me such a message. I tell you, he wouldn't dare!"

"You dunno Jack," Uncle Josh said with much meaning. "He'd do what your pa tells him to do. Don't make no mistake about that. That's a fine, set-up, young man, Sarah, and he knows what side his bread is buttered on, too."

At this, the girl cast a worried, inquisitive glance at Uncle Josh, as though she would pierce to the very heart of his meaning, but found it very hard to do so. Then she turned back to Jack Talbot who, drawing rein at such a distance that the speed of his halting would not knock a cloud of dust over the girl, threw himself out of the saddle and stepped up to the group.

"How are you, Uncle Josh?" he asked Peters, and to the girl: "Sarah, will you step aside with me for a minute?"

"Go on, Sarah," said Uncle Josh. "I told you so," he added

in a sort of bitter triumph.

"He told you what?" Talbot asked, frowning.

"That you was runnin' an errand for Mister Hampstead," said the old rancher calmly.

Here Talbot bit his lip. He stepped close to the girl, murmuring, and, in the meantime, Skinny made whispered conversation with his champion, Tom.

"What do you think of the looks of that gent that wants to marry her?"

"I dunno," answered the gloomy Tom.

"I do," said Skinny with much assurance. "He's the son of old man Harry Talbot. I heard tell about him. He was plumb set on sendin' his kid away to school. Sent him clean through Harvard or some other of them big places back East. Well, sir, he used up all his coin, busted himself, and damn' if he didn't kill himself, too, to get Jack through college. He used up his farm and had to sell it. Jack comes out of school with a pile of education and no place to live. So he goes to Hampstead, and Hampstead uses him like a sort of a straw boss, workin' right under him. They's some says that he's trainin' him to run the ranch and then marry Sarah. Ain't that the devil?"

"What's wrong with that?" Tom asked sadly. "Ain't that a good chance for him?"

"Look, here," said the logical and cold-minded Skinny. "If you was sweet on a girl, would you go and lick the boots of her dad?"

"Maybe not."

"Hmm!" grunted Skinny. "Folks ain't got no opinion of Talbot around these parts. Know what he looks like?"

"Fine lookin' gent," Tom said grudgingly.

"Sure he is. Reminds me of one of them ads in the magazines. You know . . . gloves in one hand and a cane in the other, smokin' a cigarette and lookin' at a hoss race. That's what he reminds me of. Dog-gone if a gent as fine lookin' as him mustn't be a heartbreaker."

"Sure," said Tom drearily. "Sure he must be."

"But he don't seem to be pleasin' her none now," muttered Skinny.

"No?"

"Look at her get red and stamp."

"I won't go!" the girl was exclaiming in a passion. "He . . . he shouldn't send for me like this when . . . when. . . ."

"Sarah!" broke in Talbot, and he pointed to those who stood around him.

She glanced wildly about her. Then, with a low cry of shame and of anger, she ran back to Peters and caught his hands.

"Dear old Uncle Josh," she murmured to him.

"Well, honey, was I right?"

"You were. And, oh, I wish I were a man!"

"So's you could do somethin' foolish?"

"Men have wills of their own and ways of their own. But what can a girl do . . . except simply mind?"

"I wish that they all thought the way you do," said Peters reverently. "Don't you go botherin' your head none about this. There ain't nobody that don't respect you a pile more for doin' just what your dad told you to do. Now you run along and hop back into that wagon."

She nodded, looked ruefully at him again, and then allowed herself to be conducted to the buckboard. She was no sooner in than she leaned out again to him.

"No matter what happens, you know that I love you, Uncle Josh."

"Of course, I do."

Then the buckboard started away. It passed Tom, still hat in hand, and he heard her cry: "You'll take care of Uncle Josh, Mister Jones?"

He nodded to her. Then the big form of young Jack Talbot passed by, loftily on his horse. He slowed his animal at the side of Tom for a single breathing space.

"If you've mixed into this affair, young man," he said sternly and softly, "you'd better take care of yourself and forget about Peters."

Then he touched his horse with the spurs and was off in a flash to overtake the buckboard, beside which he rode up the hill.

VII

"DEAD CENTERED"

"What did he say to you?" asked Skinny, as he and Tom rode across the fields after the cattle, now dark, small figures in the distance.

"He didn't have much time," Tom said quietly, "but he gave me a pretty good picture of himself."

"What did it look like to you?"

"Like a skunk!" said Tom with sudden savagery. "What sort of a name has this here Talbot?"

"Him? He's one of them good boys. He's studied law. They say he's a pretty good lawyer."

"Well," Tom said, still grudgingly, "that's something, I guess. Why ain't he practicin' some place or other?"

"Why should he start in at law when he can pick up a wife an' a ranch so dead easy?"

"He's gonna marry Sarah, is he?"

"That's what they tell me. You heard."

"Well, what've you got ag'in' him?" Tom asked.

"Nothin'. I guess you know . . . they's one pretty good thing about him and all his folks."

"Well?"

"All the Talbots is great fighters," said Skinny. "I've heard tell about his daddy. Old man Talbot would've fought a buzz saw mighty quick. And he'd've licked it, too. If he couldn't lick it with his hands, he'd've used a gun."

"How come a man can study law and work with a gun, too?" asked Tom curiously.

"They got rifle teams in these here colleges. He was one of them bull's-eye getters. Well, there ain't no Talbot ever been stopped around these parts."

With this he turned sidewise in his saddle and grinned broadly at his companion. But Tom did not seem to find any inference in that sparkling glance. He merely shrugged his shoulders and set out after the vanishing cows at a canter with Skinny, a fly-weight in the saddle, flying after him.

All night they ranged up and down the hills, Skinny riding one series of crests and Tom another, so that practically all of the cattle were in sight every moment of the time. It was easy work on this night, however, for the cattle had become so famished while they were penned up in the corral and kept on short rations that, when there were ample supplies of the sweet grama grass, they fed furiously and continuously, mowing all before them, stirring slowly from place to place, rather like sheep than like beeves.

The sun was not well up when they saw Josh Peters jog trotting toward them. He was full of spirits and hailed them in the greatest glee. They would beat old Hampstead in this fashion, he declared, and in so doing they would be vanquishing that formidable money-maker for the first time in his career. They were to hurry back to the shack, eat the breakfast that they would find waiting for them, and then turn in for a sleep before the blazing heat of the day began. They followed these instructions.

★ ★ ★ ★ ★

"How many times you worked before this time?" Tom asked of Skinny while they sat in the shack, devouring their rations.

"I dunno," said Skinny. "Workin' ain't my line."

"What is your line, Skinny?"

"Thinkin' is my line."

They had reached such a point in their companionship that Tom rarely laughed at Skinny's remarks any more.

"Ain't this work, Skinny? Ridin' herd all night?"

"Suppose that we meet up with those rustlers. It won't be work for me, then."

"What'll it be?"

"It'll be a show. I'll watch you saw into 'em."

"Ain't you goin' to help me, Skinny?" Tom asked, amused.

"Nope. A gent that can't save himself ain't worth much. I heard a preacher say that once."

"A preacher, Skinny."

"Anyways, he was standin' on a box in a street in some town. I forget its name. I just remember that I borrowed some fine chickens out of their yards in that same place."

The second and the third nights went off as smoothly as the first, and Tom and Skinny began to swear that the night-life was the only life worth living on the range. It was not until the fourth night, when the cows were already getting back their vigor and beginning to wander more rapidly from one part to another of their range, that the blow was struck.

Tom saw Skinny start away from his ridge, where he was making observations, and sweep down like a hawk toward him. He swung aside from his own line of travel to meet the boy.

"They're here," Skinny said with wonderful calm, swinging his horse in at the side of Tom's. "I seen four of 'em hedgin' around down the draw to cut in behind some of the cows. They seen us startin' south earlier. I guess that they didn't think we'd come back after these here strays so quick."

"What are you gonna do, Skinny?"

"Nothin'."

"Then keep back out of sight, will you?"

"If I'm out of their sight, ain't they out of mine?"

"Sure."

"Well, Tom, I'm gonna see what happens."

It was useless to argue with the boy and, besides, Tom had a half belief that no harm could come to such an imp as Skinny until the hour of his appointed death. For he was truly rather more elf than human.

From the ridge that Skinny had just abandoned, Tom easily made out the figures that the boy had mentioned. Seven cattle were being hurried to the north with four horsemen pressing close behind them. The plan of Tom was quickly made, and, being a man of action rather than of adroit calculation, his plan was simple in the extreme. It consisted, merely, in drawing a large semicircle from the place where he then was, and so cutting across the direction of flight of the fugitives.

As he rode, his heart stirred in him. He had no doubt of success, no matter what odds were against him. He had fought before this night in many an affair where the right and the wrong was a most dubious matter and hard to be judged, but on this occasion there was nothing but right on his side, and, when he considered the manner in which old Josh Peters was being robbed of his substance, his blood grew hotter still.

His rifle he unslung as he galloped, with the boy skimming his horse lightly at his side. Then Skinny swept up to the lead, with Tom shouting after him not to be a fool and throw his life away. But on went Skinny until he was a tiny form, bobbing up and down through the mist of the darkness. At length, when Tom believed that the boy must have far out ridden the line of the rustlers' retreat, he found himself gaining on the youngster at last. He came up furious, but, before he had time to speak, Skinny pointed down through the trees.

Past these black trunks, Tom could look into a hollow and see the little caravan approaching, the beeves on the run.

"I seen that you'd never cut in on them, the pace that you started," Skinny said simply.

Tom had to bite his lips and admit that the boy was right. Then he skirted swiftly through the woods until he came to their lower edge, and there he poised his rifle at his shoulder. On came the little drove with the men behind it and on either side, hurrying their charges along and keeping them to a straight line. All were black forms in the starlight.

"Halt!" yelled Tom, and fired.

He had aimed just in front of the nearest man, for he did not wish to kill. The result of the shot was that he, who must have heard the wicked voice of the bullet as it fled past him, drew in his horse with a frightened shout and then discharged a random shot from his revolver toward the trees. The three more distant horsemen fell in a swirling circle of confusion. In the meantime, the cattle, seeing a gap in the ranks of their herdsmen and hearing the *clang* of the rifle in their front, swung about and stampeded toward the rear.

They were allowed to go, as a matter of course, and the four riders scattered through the hollow, riding at a furious full speed to get to safety. They kept up a heavy, steady fire toward the trees. But Tom, contented with his work, had drawn his horse back among the trees and waited, peering out at the fugitives.

Then he heard a raging voice behind him. "Are you gonna let 'em go? Are you gonna let the whole lot of 'em get off?"

"Why should I start murderin'?" asked Tom, amazed.

"This is a devil of a show that I been waitin' to see," Skinny groaned. "Gimme the gun and I'll give you something worthwhile."

He clutched at the rifle as he spoke, and Tom, curious to see if the boy meant what he said, let him take it. Instantly the butt was jerked against the shoulder of Skinny; the long barrel grew as steady as though it were resting on a rock; the muzzle began to swing slowly as the young marksman picked up a flying target; the bird claw finger began to squeeze the trigger. Tom had seen enough. He knocked up the gun just as it exploded and pulled it back from Skinny's resisting hands.

"I had him dead centered!" wailed Skinny. "I'd've got him sure! That houn' was done for, if you hadn't bothered me!"

Into the safety of the dim distance fled the four. Then Tom turned to his youthful companion.

"D'you know what talk like that means?" he asked.

"I dunno . . . I don't care. I'd've got a scalp sure."

"Sure. If you got one, then you wouldn't be happy till you got another. Pretty soon folks would get together and give you something all free."

"What?" asked Skinny.

"A rope," explained Tom.

VIII

"SARAH IS DISCUSSED"

From Colorado to the Golden Gate there is one time in every day when the skies are clear, and that time is the coming of the evening. It begins when the sun sets, and it lasts until the final afterglow has vanished from the heart of the sky and from the edges of the horizon. It is a time of quiet. The very earth that has been burnished and burned by the sun all day now seems to suspire and enjoy the coming coolness. Voices of men that had been harsh now grow soft. People speak in murmurs. The muscles relax; the heart beats more slowly. Many and many a pound of tobacco is then burned along the verandahs of houses and small hotels. The youth slick back their hair, tie their gaudiest neckties about their throats, and sally forth to whisper in the ear of the chosen lady. All is done mildly, gently, slowly.

Mild and gentle and slow, also, was the voice of Mr. Hampstead, seated on the verandah of his ranch house, watching the big hills grow far away and turn black against the sunset.

"Won't you play something and sing something, Sarah?"

She rose without a word. Her steps passed across the porch. The screen door opened with a faint humming like a stringed instrument, and closed again with a sigh. Then the piano began to sound a few single notes, like bells, then the delicate *thrumming* of the accompaniment and the voice of the girl.

Under cover of that music, the father carried on his conversation with young Jack Talbot. They spoke in pauses, busily although softly while she sang, becoming silent when the songs ended, perhaps speaking a word of praise.

"She is steadily more and more depressed," said her father.

"I have noticed it," said Talbot.

"What do you make of the change?"

"I hardly know. . . ."

"Is it that infernal old fool, Josh Peters?"

"Yes, I think it is."

"Come, come, Jack. Speak out and let me have your thoughts. Be a man . . . I won't eat you if you disagree with me, sometimes. You mustn't act, always, as though I'm the perpetual bellwether, and that you must flock after me. Speak for yourself!"

At this, Talbot cleared his throat, collected himself, and then said, for he dreaded the rancher as a mortgaged man dreads a bank: "I'm afraid that it's a little more serious than you imagine, Mister Hampstead."

"You are, eh?"

"I am, sir."

"Drop the sir. It won't do out here in the wilds. What makes you afraid?"

"There is such a change in Sarah."

"I've told you I have noticed it."

"But it goes deeper than you think. It's more than mere depression."

"Well?"

"As though she thought that you were. . . ."

"That's it," muttered the rancher, without waiting for the sentence to be completed. "When a woman begins to think . . . the devil is to pay. Why can't they content themselves with doing what they're told to do, and let it go at that?"

In the darkness, young Talbot thrust out his jaw and nodded. "Exactly my view, Mister Hampstead."

"Still, she's obedient enough. I imagine that you haven't heard her criticizing me?"

"By no means!"

"If she did . . . ," began Hampstead sullenly, and paused with significant solemnity.

"I am sure that she would not dream of doing anything, except what you tell her to do," Talbot inserted.

"Humph!" grunted the rancher, satisfied.

"But still what she thinks. . . ."

"Damn a woman's thinking so long as it doesn't get into

her actions," said the rancher. "I want 'em in their places. That's all. As long as I have respect and obedience, she may think as much as she pleases. But about what, Jack? What's the thing on her mind?"

"I only guess, Mister Hampstead."

"Aren't you close enough to her to know her mind?"

"There are a great many things. . . . She knows that your wishes and your interests are my wishes and interests, sir."

"Well . . . well . . . well," murmured the rancher. "You're a good lad, Jack. And I've kept my eye on you. I understand how you've advanced the interests of the ranch by your work. At the same time, remember that what you do for me, you are ultimately accomplishing for yourself. With Sarah you take the ranch, also. Never forget it!"

The voice of Jack Talbot was almost inaudible with emotion. "I shall never have it out of my mind, sir," he answered with a devious conviction.

"Good!" Hampstead announced. "Now tell me everything you surmise about the girl."

"I presume that her will may be a bit more stubborn than you imagine."

"The devil! Well, go on."

"She seems to dwell on one thing a great deal."

"What is that?"

"The young fellow who is living with Josh Peters."

"That fellow Jones, eh? Tom Jones?"

"Exactly. She seems to feel that he has done a very fine thing in throwing in with Josh. She has mentioned it a hundred times to me as a sort of example of real altruism, you know. The last time I fear that I expressed a slight impatience with the subject and suggested to her that I could hardly sympathize with any man who was doing his best to balk you in your designs, sir."

"Very good, Jack. Very good, indeed. I appreciate that. And what had the minx to say to that?"

"Nothing."

"Ah! You see? Not quite lost to the sense of what is due to me, as you thought, eh?"

"But in her glance I could see that her mind was still working quietly, sir. And not working with you. I should have said something to you at the time."

"You mean?"

"That she appears to doubt the justice of your dealings with old Josh Peters."

"Damn his infernal old soul! Is money money, or is it not?"

"Of course it is, sir."

"Haven't I offered to buy him out above the market price?"

"Exactly, sir. Most generous, too. But she seems to agree with Josh that there are certain things that may not be bought, and that it is almost a sacrilege to even suggest buying them. She seems to think that old shack is a holy place to Josh . . . and that he has a right to consider it so."

"Jack, I ask you frankly if that isn't exactly like the folly of a woman?"

"Certainly, sir."

"Always hunting up obscure and foolish ideas which have no market value."

"Always, sir."

"But, between you and me, do you know what this conversation makes me determined upon?"

"I can't guess, sir."

"To do two things at once . . . smash Peters, get him out of the country, and marry you to Sarah before she progresses any further with this infernal thinking that is becoming a habit of hers. Do you understand?"

Jack Talbot choked with joy. Then he answered: "Sir, when I am the husband of your daughter, you may consider yourself as much the master of her motions as you are now."

"Humph!" said the rancher. "I hope so. I hope so. I hope that when I've made you a man and a rich man, that I'll not be entirely forgotten."

"I should be an ungrateful dog, sir, if that were the case."

"Not a word, Jack. I trust you, boy. Of all the men I've ever known . . . and I'm free to admit this to you . . . you're the only one who has been able to appreciate me. The others have called me sly, sharp, hard. You, Jack, understand that a man without some rock in him might as well be a jellyfish."

"A terrible state of affairs, sir."

"By heaven, it shall never be said of me."

"I scarcely believe so, Mister Hampstead."

"Now to get back to Peters. The old idiot has been handled tenderly long enough. He has turned himself into an armed force, so to speak. I haven't told you the details of what happened last night."

"No, sir."

"Well, Jack, I sent down a new man to run off some of old Peters's cattle. The other boys were working a little too slowly for me. They seemed afraid to undertake anything while the cows were being watched night and day. But this new fellow . . . Goodrich is his name, Jeff Goodrich . . . undertook that he would accomplish something. It seems that he actually had cut out seven or eight cows and was bringing them off successfully, when someone opened fire on them from the cover of the trees. Even by the starlight, the fellow was shooting straight. And, of course, there was nothing for Goodrich and the others to do but to bolt for cover, and the man who routed them was this same Jones. He's a thorn in our side now, this Tom Jones."

"He is, sir."

"Well, Jack, I've decided that, since they mean fighting, we'll give them a fight. And since there's to be a fight, could there be a better leader for that purpose than you, Jack?"

There was a slight pause and then the troubled voice of Talbot. "The trouble is . . . in these shooting scrapes . . . if a man should be killed. . . ."

"You mean that you might be found and punished? Trust me, lad. Trust me. Nothing would ever be found out about you. Not a word. My money is a fence between you and the law, and I know how to use it for the best effect. Consider yourself free to do as if you were back in the days of wild Indians."

Talbot drew a great, joyous breath. "Then, sir, stop worrying about Jones. He's a dead man while we're speaking."

"Take Goodrich with you. Jeff is a handy fellow, and it seems he has an old grudge against Jones. Hates him like a very devil. Take Jeff along."

"I can use a man like that, but I don't need him. Matter of fact, ever since Sarah started talking foolishly about this Jones, I've been aching to put my hands on him."

"And when that's finished, Peters is in my hands . . . and when Peters moves out and sells out . . . you marry Sarah, Jack."

IX

"JEFF GOODRICH AGAIN"

Here, as though she had been listening to the remarks and they had grown too much for her, the fingers of the girl became idle over the keys of the piano. The music ceased abruptly in the middle of a bar, and young Jack Talbot leaped to his feet in alarm.

"Do you think that she has overheard?" he asked.

"What good would it do her if she did?" responded the father, and he relighted his cigar, turning it rapidly and dexterously so that the flame of the match might ignite the whole of the charred surface of the stub. "I promise that she's my daughter, Jack, and that her future is in my hands. I presume that she herself would be the last person to question that."

Talbot, however, was still standing and listening in that frightened fashion, his heart in his throat, when it seemed to him that something stirred under the shadow of the rose bushes just in front of the verandah. He stepped to the edge of the verandah with a long, light stride, whipped out a revolver, poised it, and then murmured to the rancher: "A thieving coyote, I half believe."

With that, he fired. It seemed to him, still, that he could make out something lying flat among the shadows beneath the bushes, but since it did not stir when a gun was fired in its very ear, so to speak, he determined that his eyes must have deceived him.

How bitterly, then, he could have cursed his folly in thus firing random bullets when the sound of the revolver was followed by a wild shriek from the interior of the house. He was so stunned by the thrill of that cry that he could not move, but stood like a statue with the gun stiffly extended in his right hand.

The rancher, a squat, swift-moving form, darted past him and through the door. Before it could bang behind him, Talbot was through. They reached the living room almost together, and there they found the girl lying on her face, just at the edge of the Persian rug that made a bright patterning of color beside the piano.

Hampstead lifted her in his arms and carried her beneath the light. Her eyes were closed, her face colorless, her body limp. She had fainted. He carried her straightaway to the couch and laid her there.

"I thank the heavens it was no worse," breathed Talbot. "What a dolt I was for firing a gun like that, but I thought that I saw something or someone . . . among the shadows in the garden . . . as though listening to our talk, you understand?"

"Stop talking. You've done nothing wrong," the rancher said tersely. "Get me some water."

Talbot sped off and returned at once with a pitcher of water. He had no chance to use it. As he entered the room, he saw the girl come to life in her father's arms.

"Is he dead?" she cried hysterically. "Is he dead?"

"Is who dead? Hush . . . hush," said the rancher.

"He is! He is!" she screamed. "You're keeping the truth from me."

"Be quiet, Sarah. You're losing your nerve. Be quiet, girl. I'm here to take care of you."

"You've murdered him! You've murdered him between you!" she screamed.

"Who? Who are you afraid that we've hurt?"

"You know who I mean. I'll go to him. Let me go to him, Dad!"

"In the name of heaven, dear, what do you mean?"

"That you've killed him when he was helpless . . . that you've murdered poor Tom Jones!"

There was a gasp of horror and rage from Hampstead. "Ten thousand devils," he whispered across his shoulder to young Talbot. "What is Tom Jones to you?" he thundered to his daughter. "I'll tell you right now that I haven't seen the young rat today, which is a lucky thing for him. I haven't seen him today, but now I begin to wish to the devil that I *had* put a chunk of lead in his infernal, impudent heart! Sarah, have you gone mad? What do you mean by caring what has happened to a tramp, a penniless beggar, a man without a name? Answer me."

She brushed all the minor details away, and, slumping down on the couch, she leaned back among the pillows, one hand pressed to her heart, and smiling faintly up to her father.

"It was all a foolish fancy," she said. "But while I was playing I could hear your voice rumbling, and growing louder and louder, as if you were arguing with someone. And then . . . the gun was fired just when the thought of Tom Jones came into my mind . . . and . . . I couldn't stand it. But thank heaven that it was just a bad dream."

Hampstead was in such a silent fury that he swayed back and forth from one foot to the other, glowering at Sarah with unspeakable anger and horror. Then he stretched forth his short, bulky arm and pointed a stubby forefinger. "Go up to your room. Stay there!" he commanded.

Sarah rose, her relief turning as quickly into shrinking fear of him, and went hastily from the room.

Hampstead began to stamp up and down the room, with poor Jack Talbot making a few futile steps after him from time to time and demanding: "What's wrong? What do you think it means, sir?"

"Have you ears? Did you hear what she said?" thundered the rancher at last.

"Yes . . . yes . . . but what might it mean?"

"Are you a jackass, or are you not?"

"I hope not, sir."

"Stop sirring me. I say, when a girl faints because she thinks that a man is in danger, what does it generally infer about her sentiment toward that man?"

"Sentiments, Mister Hampstead?" cried Jack.

"By heavens, you are a fool! I mean this . . . would you guess that a girl who acts as my girl does about this Tom Jones is in love with a man or not in love?"

"Love?" groaned Jack Talbot. "Impossible!"

"Why?"

"His grammar is atrocious."

"Will bad grammar kill a woman's love?"

"I should think so. But then, a common cowpuncher. Besides, the fellow has no prospects, as far as we can make out. And, above all, she has hardly seen him."

"Do you know how long I'd known my wife when we were married?"

"A reasonable time, sir, I presume."

"One week, young man!"

"Good heavens, Mister Hampstead."

"Well, sir, I'll tell you what did it. I was a young chap bound for the West, full of courage, full of self-confidence, expecting a lot harder fight with Indians and crooks and gunmen than I actually had. That idea appealed to my wife, God bless her. Of course, she was one woman in ten million. In fact, there was never her like before. And yet her blood is in my girl, Sarah. She is soft as silk, easy as a child to handle, and yet she may have a spark in her. I remember three years ago when that big chestnut gelding bucked her off, and she landed on her head. She was unconscious for five minutes, and then she jumped up and insisted on taking another chance with the horse. I let her do it. I wanted to see her spunk. And she had enough to stay in the saddle that second time she tried it. Well, Jack, I'm telling you this in order that you may know what you have before you."

Jack Talbot stood in a corner of the room, his head bowed and his face black.

"What are you thinking of?" asked the rancher suddenly.

"I was thinking," Jack responded with the greatest deliberation, "that I have a double reason, now, for disposing of young Tom Jones. Why not tonight as well as any other time?"

"Why not?" said the rancher. "You can find Jeff easily enough. Ask Harry Shay to bring Jeff to you."

So Jack Talbot went hurriedly out from the house and found Shay in the bunkhouse. In response to the request of Talbot, the latter went out into the night and returned in twenty minutes with one of the biggest and the roughest men whom Talbot had ever seen. The grimness of the features of this fellow was accentuated by the marks of actual battering that were on his face. There was a huge mark of dull purple around his right eye. There was a livid streak beneath the left. His nose was markedly swollen, and there were some small black-and-blue spots around the point of his chin.

"You're Jeff Goodrich, are you?" asked Talbot.

"I'm him, and you're Talbot."

"That's it. Jeff, I have a little party ahead of me tonight. I want you to join me."

"I ain't interested in parties," said Goodrich.

"What is the thing you most want?"

"To hunt down a skunk. . . ."

"Named Tom Jones?"

"Aye!" Goodrich cried, his voice trembling with his emotion. "You've named him right quick and plumb easy. That's the gent that I want to get. That's him that I got to get."

"Why," Talbot explained, "that's what my party is tonight."

"To get him? To get Jones?" gasped out Goodrich.

"Exactly!"

"Mister Talbot, will you count me in?"

"That's why I've sent for you. Will the two of us be enough?"

"Lemme at him alone. Lemme have a chance to square up

things between him and me. There won't be no need for anybody else."

"Jeff," said Talbot solemnly, "he has to die. You understand?"

"Yes, damn him!" said the big man through his teeth.

"What you get out of it. . . ."

"Gimme a fast horse to ride. That's all I want. I don't want no pay. Gimme a hoss to make my getaway on. That's all!"

"I can count on you, then?"

"Shake, Talbot!"

As the horny fingers of the ruffian grated against his palms, Talbot knew that he had made a partnership in crime.

X
"A QUARTER THAT'S TALKIN' "

After Talbot had fired that shot among the rose bushes, and had run into the house in the direction of Sarah's scream, the shadow at which he had aimed rose from the ground where it had lain flat, disentangled itself from among the shrubs, and stole straight toward the now empty verandah. There, through an open window, the stealthy little form peered into the room where Sarah lay unconscious on the floor, and the light that poured through the window from the lamps illumined the wizened features of Skinny.

He watched and he listened while the girl was revived. He heard her frantic exclamations. He watched her as she was sent to her room. He listened, still, to the brief and pointed dialogue between the rancher and Talbot. Then he retreated softly over the porch, passed down the steps, and was presently lost in the night.

Among the thicket of trees farther down the hillside, he found his tethered horse, mounted, clapped his heels against the ribs of the old mustang, and rattled away for the Peters ranch. There, among the outlying hills, he came upon the grazing cattle as they strayed here and there. Upon a knoll, commanding their movements, was the guardian of the herd, Tom Jones.

The latter greeted him with no enthusiasm. "You been playin' hooky again," Tom said.

"This is gettin' dull on this here ranch," declared Skinny.

"Wasn't there enough action last night to suit you?"

"You call that action?" inquired Skinny sneeringly. "I heard a lot of noise, but I didn't see nothin' happen."

"You're a fool kid," Tom said calmly. "You'll see that Hampstead will keep his hands off after that."

"You think so?"

"I know so."

"I'll make a little bet with you, Tom. I got a quarter here that says you'll have trouble again."

"Maybe . . . sometime."

"Right tonight."

At this, Tom turned sharply upon him. "What you mean?" he said.

"Nothin' much, except that skunk Jeff Goodrich is workin' with Hampstead now, and him and Talbot is comin' down here tonight to get you, Tom."

"You're bluffin' me, Skinny."

"Maybe. I got a quarter that's talkin', though."

"By Jupiter!" exclaimed the cowpuncher, twisting about in the saddle so that he squarely confronted his small partner. "You been up the hill, and you listened in on 'em?"

"Sure."

"Well," Tom said quietly, "I guess you know, then. Which way are they aimin' to come?"

"I dunno. Except that they mean to get to work tonight."

"Skinny, you're worth your weight in greenbacks."

"Thanks. Goin' back to the house?"

"If they miss me tonight," mused the rider, "they'll sure come back and lay for me again. Nope. I think that I'll wait right out here for 'em."

"Good for you, Tom. I knowed that you had something in you! How'll you aim to handle 'em?"

"Lemme think," Tom mumbled thoughtfully. "Gimme time."

"Say," broke in Skinny, "Miss Hampstead and you has been meetin' private, some place, I guess."

"What!"

Then came the details of the story, and all that he had heard and seen. Before he ended, Tom Jones was like a man possessed.

"But it ain't possible," he said. "All it means is that she's sorry to see anybody gettin' a crooked deal. It's because I'm a friend to Peters that she's friendly to me . . . don't you think so, Skinny?"

"Sure," chuckled Skinny. "That's all."

He laughed as Tom sighed heavily. For a full half hour they argued back and forth over the possibilities of the best manner in which they could meet the attack of the two.

"But," said Skinny finally, "we got to do something. They'll be here any minute, if Talbot is goin' to act quick. And he sure looked as though he meant business after he found out that Miss Hampstead was sort of gone on you, Tom."

"We'll hit out for the woods," Tom said, and they started at a brisk canter toward the distant blackness of the forest.

They had not covered a quarter of a mile before, against the stars of the sky, they saw two horsemen riding over the brow of a hill straight before them—two horsemen who no sooner sighted them than they put spurs to their horses and charged furiously down upon the man and the boy.

"Get off your hoss . . . drop flat on the ground!" cried Tom. "The cur dogs'll shoot for you, too! Quick, Skinny!"

But no such cautious measures for safety were in the head-long brain of the boy. With a wild yell, he waved his hat in the air and thrashed it against the flank of the mustang. Then he pulled out a six-shooter that over-weighed his fragile hand, and with the horse running at full speed, he charged straight up the slope at the advancing pair.

Tom Jones, frantic with the horror and the folly of the move, followed as fast as he could. And, just as he had sus-pected, so it happened. With the revolver of the youngster snapping and barking in their faces, the two drew their own weapons. Half a dozen shots rattled through the clear, still air of the night, and then Skinny pitched to one side out of the saddle and fell headlong upon the ground.

After that, the scene was bathed in a reddish haze for Tom Jones, and the stars whirled before his eyes. He fixed his spurs in the tortured sides of his horse and sent the poor beast ahead at a furious pace. In an instant he was upon them. He fired twice at Talbot, who was riding in the lead. And twice he missed. He received a stunning blow in the left shoulder, and instantly his left arm was limp and hanging uselessly at his side. But he caught his reins in his teeth, changed his aim to Goodrich, and at the first discharge brought that warrior out of his saddle.

Then he was shot past Talbot, so near that he could see the pallor and the contortion of the face of the big youth. He controlled his mount as well as he could, swung around, and advanced to reach Talbot again. But there was no Talbot to meet. That hero, having swung his own fine mount around, took stock of the situation, saw his ally lying prone and helpless on the ground, and saw that the odds had changed to man to man. Of the dangling, helpless arm of Tom he could not be sure in the dimness of the starlight. Certainly the time that Talbot had spent in college had not been wasted. He reasoned with beautifully flawless logic that, if he and Goodrich, fighting together, had not been able to down this tigerish fellow who now rushed to the attack again, he alone would have a very small chance, indeed. Accordingly, he did not waste a moment, but, putting the spurs to his Thoroughbred, he was away from the spot as though on wings.

Tom Jones did not pursue. He rode with full speed back to the spot where Skinny had fallen and arrived just in time to see the youth stagger to his feet and reel about in a circle, holding his hand to his head.

"Skinny!" cried Tom. "Not the head! They didn't get you there?"

"Shut up!" gasped out Skinny. "Gimme time to get my wind. They bounced a slug off my head, but it didn't hurt me none."

Tom was out of the saddle and beside him. He scratched a match and by that light examined the long gash on the side of Skinny's head. It was merely a grazing wound as the boy had said, and aside from the loss of blood, that gave it an ugly appearance, it was harmless enough. So, relieved to such a point that the pain of his own wound seemed nothing, he left Skinny to construct his own bandage. In the meantime, he hurried to the place where Goodrich lay.

He found that hero writhing and groaning on the ground. And he had cause for lamentation. The .45 caliber bullet had torn its way through the thick flesh of his right thigh, keeping on the outside of the bone, but making an ugly wound, as Tom could see when he cut away the trouser leg.

He himself was helpless, with his one hand, to make a

tourniquet, but under his instruction the omnipresent Skinny, who had already joined him, accomplished that difficult bit of work. The bleeding was stopped. Goodrich's groaning subsided. Then Tom, his own head swimming with pain, kneeled beside the stricken man.

"Goodrich," he said, "you're gonna write out in full all about who sent you down here and why they sent you. Understand? Otherwise, Skinny and me start back for the shack and leave you here."

"For God's sake," moaned the other, "don't leave me. I'll tell you everything. It was all Hampstead, damn him. It was all Hampstead."

XI

"THE THIRD PERSON"

Through the morning haze, old Josh Peters jogged his down-headed mustang up the hill and over the crest and so came in view of the great house of the rich rancher. There he paused as though to take stock of himself and his powerful enemy. But although the spectacle seemed to abash him at first, he presently nodded as though in greater surety, loosened the reins, and kicked his mustang along.

He passed through the tall, wooden gate and up the drive to the hitching rack that extended in front of the old-fashioned house that had a front, indeed, more like a small Western hotel than like a private dwelling. At the rack he tethered the horse, then climbed the front steps, and rapped at the door. The Negro servant had no sooner caught sight of him than there was a frightened—"Laws a-massy!"—and with staring eyes the colored woman fled down the hall without waiting to hear the errand of the old man.

So Josh Peters sat down on a chair, drew out his old black

pipe, and had loaded and lighted it before he heard a familiar brisk step come down the verandah on the outside of the house. He looked up as the screen door banged and jangled, and there he saw beside him the master of the house, Hampstead himself.

One could not have told that there was any weight of trouble on the mind of Hampstead. His forehead was as unfurrowed as the brow of a child, and his eyes were as calm as the eyes of a grazing steer. He greeted Josh Peters with perfect indifference and cordiality, skillfully mingled.

"Josh," he said, "I suppose this little visit means that you've come to your senses and decided to sell."

Josh Peters looked upon him with a sort of quiet wonder and admiration.

"Maybe it does," he said. "You got a persuadin' way about you. But first I got a little favor to ask of you."

"Fire away, Josh."

"Lemme see that young gent that's been up here courtin' Sarah an' making love to your ranch."

"Do you mean young Jack Talbot?"

"That's him that I mean."

"What do you want with him?"

"I got to talk to him about a couple of things before I sell out to you, Hampstead."

Hampstead cleared his throat and watched his guest with a peculiar hidden caution. "Talbot has been called away."

"Sure," said Peters. "I'd been thinkin' that maybe he'd get a call like that. He was called home, wasn't he?"

"Why . . . I believe so."

"They ain't no chance that you'd know where his home is, is they?"

"As a matter of fact, he left no address. He was in a hurry, but he'll be back soon."

69

"Not so soon, maybe," Peters commented.

"I don't know what you mean," Hampstead said with magnificent indifference.

"You don't, eh?"

"Certainly not. What are you hinting at, Josh? What idea is in your head?"

Josh Peters rocked back in his chair and nodded amiably at his companion. "Dog-gone me," he said, "they ain't no doubt but what you're a great man, Hampstead. They ain't nobody like you. Nobody at all!"

Hampstead bit his lip. "All of this means what?"

"I got a friend of Talbot's down at my house. He's frettin' a lot, he's so plumb anxious to see young Jack."

"What friend do you speak of?"

"A gent that I guess you never heard of. His first name is Jeff."

"Jeff who?"

"Well, he says that he knows you, but I gathered that you'd be apt to disremember him. I see that I was right. He says that he knows you pretty well, though, Hampstead. Says he's been on your payroll, as a matter of fact."

"The man is mad," replied the rancher calmly. "Besides, what is he to me?"

"My son used to be readin' law all the time," Josh said, yawning.

"Well, what about it?"

"He tried to talk to me about his books. Lookin' back to what he used to tell me about things, I'd say that this here Jeff could have you up for bein' a party to a murder scheme. I mean he could have you up with him."

"I don't in the least know what you're talking about, but as far as I can guess, there seems to be a blackmail scheme in your mind, Josh. Come, come! You're too honest a fellow for that. Come right out and tell me what you want and who's been filling your mind full of this nonsense."

"I don't mind talkin' straight from the shoulder," the old man assured him. "Matter of fact, that's my most favorite way of doin' things. I'll tell you what I'll do. You pay me for all the cows that have been stole from my ranch, and you lay off my ranch. Then all you got to do is settle up with young Tom Jones and this here Jeff. That's about the way I look at it. You satisfy me first, and then I lay off you. Now talk turkey, Hampstead."

Something that had been closely confined in Hampstead, but gaining in force all of the time, now exploded. It turned out to be the most violent wrath.

"You infernal old villain!" he thundered. "This is blackmail! And you're the man they call honest Josh Peters!"

Honest Josh Peters raised his hand. "Talk soft, Hampstead," he said, "or else I'll have to read out loud in a big voice all the things that's wrote down here in this paper." He drew it from his pocket.

"What's on that paper?" asked Hampstead, suddenly grown husky of throat.

"Nothin' except the proofs that you, Hampstead, have been rustlin' my cows and that you, Hampstead, tried your damned best to get my man Tom Jones murdered. Understand? That's all they is in this here paper. Take a look at it. Take your time, they ain't no hurry."

Hampstead snatched the paper and ran his eye swiftly over it. Then he read the paper through again, slowly, carefully.

"Very well," he said, folding it and handing it back. "I hope you take this to a lawyer. He'll tell you that you haven't a chance of doing a thing with this in a court of law. Understand me?"

"You ain't going to let me get to no lawyer, Hampstead,"

71

said the old man calmly. "What you're goin' to do is talk turkey to me right here and now. Hampstead, you been boss of the roost for a good many years. You've squeezed a lot of others. You've tried to squeeze me. Now I've got you in my hands, and I'm going to do some of that same kind of squeezin'."

"I believe that you'd do your best," said Hampstead furiously. "As for this tissue of foolish lies . . . let the fool attempt to prove that he was hired by me to kill Jones. As a matter of fact, what happened was that the two met on the range and had a gunfight. Then they decided to try to frame me . . . between them. But it won't work, Peters. Not while my money can hire good lawyers to defend my innocence."

"They ain't the only witnesses," said Peters.

"Who else, then?"

"Why, there's your young friend, that's to marry your girl. There's young Jack Talbot."

"Talbot!" exploded the rancher hotly. But he added at once: "What has he to do with it?"

"He was along. That's all. He was one of them that made the attack."

"Nonsense! A conspiracy between this Jeff Goodrich and Jones. No court of law would believe such a thing. A young fellow like Talbot . . . eminently respectable and engaged to my daughter."

Josh Peters inquired curiously: "How come you to let a yaller houn' dog get engaged to Sarah?"

"No more of that, Josh."

"Well, didn't he cut and run while the set-to was goin' on, the pup."

Hampstead smote his hands together in mute agony, and the beaded perspiration was on his forehead. "Go on with your case. I say nothing can be proved against Talbot."

"They's still another witness, Hampstead."

"Well? Well? Will this thing never end? Who's the third person?"

"A kid called Skinny, with no last name. He was what brought Tom Jones to me and saved my goose. And last night, he come up here and lay down in the rose garden, yonder, while you and young Jack Talbot was talkin' pretty free together. . . ."

"Ten thousand devils!" shouted Hampstead. "I wish that Talbot had killed the brat."

"I ain't wishin' the same thing," said Josh gravely. "Afterward, he slips up on the porch when you and Jack was tryin' to bring Sarah back out of her faintin' fit. He heard you and Jack talk and plan the whole thing. . . ."

There was a groan from Hampstead, and then: "Who'll believe the chatter of a child, under age?"

"Everybody in these here mountains will, Hampstead. He's got a bullet mark along the side of his head that your same young friend Talbot fired at him. I tell you, Hampstead, that folks knows that a kid that has the nerve to stand up and take gunfire has got the nerve to tell the truth, too."

Hampstead fell into a chair so hard that it shuddered beneath him. "It's this rat of a fellow . . . this damned rat . . . Tom Jones . . . he's forced me into this devilish hole," he groaned.

"Well, Hampstead, here I am talkin' business. Do I get the price of them cows that you stole from me?"

"Damn you! Yes, Josh, you get every penny. Understand, man, I always intended to see that you did not suffer, if I couldn't squeeze you out. It wasn't that I wanted to rob you. It was only because I needed that land, and. . . ."

"Hampstead," said the old man gently, "I thank God that there wasn't no killin' done last night. Since there wasn't, I can afford to remember that you're the father of Sarah. Otherwise . . . I'd've had you in prison for this, and you'd've been run out of the country when you got through servin' your term."

XII

"IVORY TEMPERED WITH MEANNESS"

That morning, in the shack of Josh Peters, the controlling hand was that of Skinny. The bandage that he wore around his head was no more than a sort of a badge of office. Around his hips there was girdled a large cartridge belt that fell almost to his knees, and from the belt there sagged still lower the holster of the Colt revolver, well nigh dragging on the floor. But this unhandy weapon was necessary, because Skinny was now acting in a treble capacity as nurse, cook, and guardian of the house. And, although his face was pale and drawn, his eyes were brighter than ever, and went everywhere at once.

He was carrying in a plate of ham and eggs to the sufferers. These lay side by side on the bed of Josh Peters. The doctor had come to dress their wounds afresh and bandage the hurt on the head of Skinny, whose skull he had pronounced harder than steel itself.

"Ivory tempered with meanness," Tom Jones had said, grinning.

They greeted the food with enthusiasm, and, when the head of Jeff had been propped groaningly high enough to eat, the meal proceeded, while Skinny sat on the foot of the bed and regarded them—the face of Goodrich with scorn and hatred—the face of Tom Jones with unspeakable love and idolatry.

Yet, being a gentleman at all times, he allowed not a hint of his true emotions to appear in either his words or in his actions. He was all good cheer.

"Peters has gone up to see old man Hampstead," he said. "There must be a lot of noise and trouble bustin' around loose up yonder about this time of the day."

"He'll pay me!" Goodrich exclaimed. "He'll pay me for sendin' me out with a skunk that quit me when I got in a pinch. He'll pay me, and he'll pay me good and plenty!"

A quick glance was interchanged between the boy and Tom Jones, but they said not a word. It was not for them to criticize the mental or the moral ways of a helpless enemy who was in their hands.

"How's your leg, Jeff?" asked Skinny.

"Bad! They ain't no way that I can lie easy without puttin' no weight on it. It near kills me. I dunno why the doctor didn't give me something to make the pain stop. He might've give me a slug of morphine, or something."

"Too bad," Skinny said sympathetically. "And how you comin', Tom, old man?"

"Doin' fine. They ain't no bones busted. I'll be around in a few days. I could walk fine right now if. . . ."

Although the words brought the thought to full fruition in his mind at that instant, he leaped from the bed and raised his hand for silence. Outside the house the rattle of horses' hoofs had come to a sudden halt, and then a small, gentle voice was heard, speaking to the animal.

"It's her," breathed Tom.

"It's who?" asked Goodrich.

"Shut up!" Skinny commanded savagely, forgetting his courtesy for the nonce. "It's her!"

She came eagerly through the door of the room and went to Tom, blind to all else. "Oh, Tom," she said to him, "when they told me that you had been hurt, and that . . . and that . . . I thought that I'd have to come . . . because . . . but you're going to get well, aren't you?"

"I ain't more'n scratched," Tom answered, his eyes wild with happiness. "Fact is, I ain't hurt at all . . . just come along out of this here room. It's so dog-gone hot and close. . . ."

They disappeared through the doorway.

"The doc'll give him the devil for gettin' up and walkin' around like that," Goodrich said glumly to the boy, while he turned his curious eyes toward the empty doorway.

"D'you see her? Ain't she a queen?" gasped out Skinny.

"I've seen a pile of girls that was better lookin'."

"The devil you have!" Skinny responded. He stirred restlessly to the door, back again, and then stole out into the shack.

He was gone for a long time. When he returned, his face was very red and his eyes were shining.

"What's happened?" Goodrich asked gruffly.

"Nothin'," snapped out Skinny. "Nothin' at all. Jiminy . . . !"

"Jiminy . . . what?"

"You'd ought to have seen."

Skinny walked up and down the room, unable to contain himself.

"What was it, Skinny?"

"I never seen nothin' like it."

"Like what?"

"I'll see you go to the devil before I tell!" Skinny shouted, losing his thin-drawn temper.

There fell a sullen silence in that room, while Skinny walked nervously and hastily to and fro. Then a door opened somewhere in the house. Skinny stopped, his head raised to listen. And they could both hear her voice—how changed and deepened and strengthened it was.

"I'll ride up home as fast as I can. And then I'll be back

with things you must have . . . dear Tom."

The rumble of Tom's voice was an unintelligible thunder. They were gone to the front of the house.

"I knowed it," Skinny whispered calmly, sinking into a chair. "Everything had to come out all right in the end. This gent Talbot, he might've beat Tom, but he couldn't beat Tom when he was hooked up with me."

Sleeper Pays a Debt

"Sleeper Pays a Debt" appeared in the second issue, dated October, 1934, of the short-lived pulp publication, *Mavericks*. It was one of five stories Frederick Faust wrote about his hero named Sleeper, a character with many similarities to another of his creations, Reata, whose stories had appeared a year earlier in Street & Smith's *Western Story Magazine*. Both are loners, temporarily beholden to a peddler, in both cases known as Pop, and neither carry a gun, although both are adept at outsmarting their enemies—Sleeper with a knife and Reata with a lariat. "One Man Posse," the first Sleeper story, chronologically, can be found in *Timber Line: A Western Trio* (Five Star Westerns, 1999). The last two Sleeper stories—"Inverness" and "Death in Alkali Flat"—are collected in *More Tales of the Wild West* (Circle V Westerns, 1999). The Sleeper saga will be complete with the publication of "Satan's Gun Rider" in *Joker's Extra Wild* (Five Star Westerns, 2002).

I

"ROARING WATER"

Something was wrong. Sleeper had noticed nothing unusual from the higher land, but as soon as he reached the low ground beside Crazy Horse Creek, he felt a tremor through the earth and a quivering in the air, or was it only a tension in his own nerves, a sudden, inexplicable warning that freighted the hot midday—a thing of the mind rather than of the body?

He slipped from the back of the bright chestnut stallion. He looked in his ragged, patched rig like some vagabond grub-line rider that might have stolen the great horse. Now, rising in his stirrups and scanning the horizon on all sides, he saw nothing at all.

On the edge of the horizon toward White Water there was a small cloud. Otherwise the sky was a clear basalt blue. The sound that he had heard or felt, could it be thunder rolling from that small cloud so near the horizon? He shook his head, brow puckering. No sense to that. Yet, there was something. . . .

He stretched himself flat on the earth and pressed his ear to it. There was no vibration, no sound transmitted. The golden chestnut put down his head anxiously, and snuffed at the ground beside his master. Sleeper caught him by the mane and so was swept to his feet as the stallion tossed his head. He continued that movement, with a slight spring that brought him right into the saddle. Then he rode Careless straight into the creek.

The stallion had seemed perfectly unconcerned while it was on dry ground, but as soon as it entered the water, it showed every sign of fear, flattening its ears and looking repeatedly toward the bend of the creek, upstream.

"What the devil's the matter, Careless?" asked Sleeper.

The horse rolled his bright eyes back as though he wished to make answer, and at the same time pressed forward across the stream. The stallion was well into the middle, the current sweeping up about the glossy shoulders, when a change of the wind blew a definite sound of thunder toward Sleeper. And then a moment later, looking upstream, he saw the cause of it.

A wall of water six feet high was sweeping around the bend. It was almost as straight as masonry, except for its angry yellow foam on top and the tree trunks and débris tumbling there, and the thousands of tons of lunging current pushing behind it. It had not made enough noise to send its voice before it against the wind, but now that the air changed, it sent a sound like the distant thunder of a trail herd's hoofs. It was as though nature, like a murderer, knife in hand, had crept up behind her victim and was now in leaping distance, ready to strike.

Veering about the curve, that wall of water sheered off the bank as though with the stroke of a vast shovel. Some big cottonwoods were jerked down into the current, buried. One of them leaped up again, showing all its length like a living thing that strove to escape from torture.

The wave came fast. Far away in the hills a cloudburst must have dropped into the upper valley, and now its burden was rushing softly through the lower land. And now that it had appeared, as though casting all caution to the wind, it shouted aloud. So a lion might roar as it leaps for the kill, paralyzing every sense in the helpless prey. So a grizzly thunders as it rises to strike down a prime beef.

But Sleeper was not paralyzed. He cast one look behind him toward the bank he had left. The distance behind him was greater than that which lay ahead. Also, time would be lost in the turning. So he called to Careless through the tumult, and the stallion lunged furiously ahead. He must have sensed the danger from afar, and now he fought with a human eagerness for his life and that of his master. If it had been all shallow water, he would have rushed through to the safety of the farther shore. Instead, he was plunged, swimming, into water higher than his head.

Sleeper, slipping instantly into the stream, swam powerfully beside him. He could have gained on the stallion and reached the shore in safety, perhaps, but he had no thought of that. He would as soon have thought of abandoning a portion of his own body as of leaving Careless behind him.

The wave rushed on them. It was sweeping closer. Already a strange tremor broke the surface of the creek into a tiny dance of waves. They would be caught; they would be hurled down the stream. Over the head of the wall of water, Sleeper saw the heavy butt end of a tree trunk lifting, lurching toward him. A fall from a cliff could not have given more certain promise of death.

Then—it was not that he heard the shouting of the man's voice through the tumult, but because an instinct made him look up—Sleeper saw a horseman on the bank toward which he struggled. A lean man of the desert on a desert mustang, all rawhide and bones. And the stranger was swinging a rope, ready for the cast.

Sleeper, with a waved arm, gave signal that he was ready. The rope shot out, landed in Sleeper's grasp, and the noose was instantly over the horn of the saddle.

"Not the horse, you fool!" the man on horseback shouted. "I can't pull the horse in . . . too heavy . . . grab the rope for yourself!"

Although he heard the voice faintly but clearly, Sleeper would not change his mind or the grip of the rope. They would live together or die together, he and Careless.

Looking up, Sleeper saw the towering face of the wall of dull water high above him. The uproar grew immense. On the shore the rider, positioning his horse back on its haunches to receive the pull, was taking a dally around the saddle horn, ready to turn it loose if the strain threatened to engulf him and his pony in the swirling cascade.

The rope caught hard on Careless' pommel. His head

moved upstream. Struggling with all his might, the force of the stream now helped to sway him with the strain of the lariat toward the shore. He had hoofs on the shoaling ground when the edge of the rolling wall struck him and rolled him. Sleeper, casting himself ahead, gripped the rope just before the nose of the stallion and rolled with him in the same terrible confusion.

The sky flashed over his head—was lost—flashed again as he bit at the air for life-giving breath. The rope trembled with the frightful strain. The trunk of a small tree leaped past him like a dark snake.

Then in an instant the danger was gone, and they were drawn from the edge of the monstrous wave up on the high, dry bank. There the desert rider began to pull in his loosened rope and methodically coil it. Water had swept as high as the shoulders of his mustang. But now that the peril was past, he seemed as calm as though he had done no more than rope a calf at the branding pen.

Careless, safe at last, unharmed, polished to a burning copper with water and sunlight, turned and sent a great neigh of defiance after the rush of the wave.

That wall of water was speeding fast down the valley. It turned the curve below, and the thunder of it was gone. There was only the sloshing sound of the following water, and the noise of sucking as the dry sand drank up the stream.

Sleeper shook some of the water from him and went up to the stranger. The man's sunburned face was leather-dark, and his faded eyebrows were only pale marks against the skin. There seemed to be a permanent dust settled in the wrinkles about the eyes and the mouth. A face as long and lean as the body of the man, a tired face, but the eyes were filled with restless life.

Sleeper held out his hand. "Thanks," he said.

His hand was taken in a dry, quick grasp. The palm of the stranger felt like rough paper. "That's all right, kid," he said. "One of them near things, though."

"We'd be dead as hell if you hadn't stuck to your place," remarked Sleeper, beginning to strip off his soaking clothes.

"That horse belong to you?" asked the stranger, running his glance over the matchless lines of the great stallion. "Or you taking it some place for your boss?"

"Taking it some place for my boss," said Sleeper. "Only I'm the boss." He smiled and explained: "I've got a claim on Careless, but he's got a claim on me, too."

"Yeah?" drawled the man. "What's your name, kid?"

"Sleeper."

"Bones is what most of the boys call me," volunteered the rider. "What price would you put on this horse?"

"I'm not selling him."

"Better put a price on him," urged Bones. "He'd be useful to a man in a pinch. And I'm that man."

"Not selling," Sleeper answered shortly. He had his clothes off and was beginning to wring them out. Dressed, he looked as though he would strip as lean as a plucked crow. Instead, the rounded depth of his chest was a surprise, and his arms and legs were round, also, with an intricate rippling of lithe muscles. Every part of his body had the supple strength of a cat's forearm. But the glance of Bones was for the horse, not for the man.

"Kid," he said, "I wouldn't want to beat you down. I'd pay five hundred for a horse like that."

"He's been sold for a thousand," said Sleeper.

Bones flushed. "I'm paying five hundred," he said. "Maybe I'll send you some more later on."

"Thanks," said Sleeper, "but he's not for sale."

"The mustang and five hundred bucks," persisted Bones

in a low voice. He dismounted and went to the head of Care-less. "I'm sorry, Sleeper," he said. "But I need a good horse, right now. I got a real need for him."

"I'd lend him to you till you're through the pinch," said Sleeper.

"Lending be damned, I want to own him. Here's the money. Take that or take nothing!"

II
"BLOOD MONEY!"

Sleeper, stretching out his hand for the money, laid his grasp lightly on the wrist of Bones. By that touch he read the whole body of the tall man. There might be a hundred and eighty pounds in that bony frame, and by the stiffness of the tendons in the wrist he was muscled like a mule. Not an ounce of fat on him. He was tough as rawhide all the way through.

"Too bad, mister," said Sleeper. "I'm not selling."

"You poor fool!" Bones sneered. "Then you get the mustang . . . an' that's all." He tried to pull away his hand containing the money, but the grasp of Sleeper held it. "Why . . . damn you!" cried Bones, jerking his hand. He had a gun at his hip, but he didn't try to use it against this unarmed kid. Instead, he tried a blow that had begun and ended many a fight for him in the line camp, bunkhouse, and trail-town brawl wherever he had traveled on the rough way of his life. It was a neat, chopping, overhand right that would glide over a man's guard and drop like the blow of a loaded whip butt on the jaw. Now, because he was impatient, he forgot the slight-ness of the figure of this younger man and lashed out with his full strength.

Very slightly Sleeper shifted. The crushing blow brushed the skin of his cheek and seemed to spin him about. Sleeper's left hand, reaching up like the dart of a snake's head as he turned his back on Bones, caught the striking fist at the wrist and pulled it down over his shoulder. Then he doubled over, and Bones's lanky weight shot into the air, landing on the sand in a rolling fall.

The mustang tossed its head and ran a short distance away. The golden stallion came closer with bright, inquisitive eyes. But Bones did not rise at once. He lay flat on his back, stunned, and stared at the sun, while Sleeper removed the six-gun from its holster. Then he reached inside the loose gap of the man's flannel shirt for the braided strands of horsehair from which there was suspended a small double-barreled Derringer. He took it. After this, he stepped back and sat down on a rock and tossed both guns a little distance away onto the sand.

When Bones sat up, he found Sleeper playing with a hunting knife that he was tossing into the air and catching by the point on his thumb as the knife whirled down. It was a heavy knife, and the point of it was so thin that it was a mere streak of light. Sleeper's clothes had been spread out to dry on the rock beside him.

"Where'd you learn that trick?" asked Bones, without grudge or passion.

"I know a Chinaman up in the hills," said Sleeper. "He's pretty nearly fifty, but he's still faster than a flash with his hands. He does queer things. You grab him, and he makes your own weight beat you. I've worked for years with him." He yawned and stretched, letting the knife sink down into the sand, so that only the top of its handle appeared above the surface. "When I'm not trying his tricks, I'm thinking about them," Sleeper continued. "Tricks like his take a whole lot of thinking." Finding his clothes were drying too slowly, he shook them out in the sun again.

Bones rose and rolled a cigarette. "You're a better man than I am . . . with your hands," he said calmly.

"Sorry," said Sleeper. "But I knew the sand was pretty soft and would break the fall. Otherwise, it would have snapped your left shoulder, maybe."

"You mean that you've really worked out this game till you know what will happen every lick of the time?"

"Pretty much. I don't know as much as old Sam Wu, but I know something. He still has a lot to teach me, but I keep on learning."

"I'd like to take some wrestling lessons from him," Bones advised.

"It's not wrestling. It's a way of living, too. You have to learn to stand pain and look as though you like it. That's one of those things that you have to start when you're pretty young. It teaches you to relax." Sleeper grinned and stretched and yawned again. "That's the lesson that I learned the best," he said.

Bones rubbed his left shoulder thoughtfully. "I've missed something," he muttered.

"I told you before that you could have Careless as a loan," said Sleeper. "Why don't you take him? He'll carry you clean away from the sheriff."

"Who said anything about a sheriff?" asked Bones.

"Well, the dead men didn't tell me," Sleeper responded, smiling. "Neither of them said a word."

Bones, growing slightly pale, took a stealthy step forward.

"It's all right," said Sleeper. "I'm no bounty hunter. I don't want blood money."

"By God!" exclaimed Bones. "They couldn't have posted the reward this far away, as quick as all this?"

"They didn't post any reward."

"How d'you know . . . I mean . . . damn it, kid, who are you, anyway?"

"I'm a friend," Sleeper answered with a sudden gravity. He rose and held out his hand.

Bones took it with a gingerly grasp. "All right," he said.

"Say the same thing to me," went on Sleeper, "and you're welcome to those guns."

Bones hesitated for an instant. The word was apparently an important one to him, but finally he muttered: "*Bueno,* we're friends. But damned if this don't beat me."

"Come along," said Sleeper. "You ought to be on your way, and we'll talk while we ride. You won't take Careless?"

Bones pulled out a bandanna and wiped his forehead. "I need to make miles," he said, "but if I borrow Careless, you'll never see him again."

"He owes you his life, and I owe you mine," said Sleeper. "It was only when you said that you were going to *take* him that I couldn't stand it."

"I was buying him."

"A million wouldn't buy Careless. But can you ride him? Some can't."

"I'll try him." He walked to the place where his guns lay, picked them up, and blew the sand out of them. As he handled the weapons, he cast a grim glance toward Sleeper. Then he put them away, and went to the golden stallion. "It's the first time in my life that I ever took something for nothing," he said.

"You're welcome," said Sleeper. He took a great breath and looked down at the ground.

"What's his style?" asked Bones.

Sleeper had to pause before he could force himself to answer. "He'll do a little fence-rowing," he answered. "Then he's likely to sunfish. And sometimes he falls over backward, and gets up with a jump. But the worst part is . . . that he'll start whirling anytime. And he comes out of the whirl by throwing himself at the ground and flopping over sideways."

"My God," said Bones, "how does *anybody* ride him? And where did he learn all those tricks?"

"I've been teaching him a little," Sleeper admitted. "But maybe he can be ridden still. Wait a minute." He went up to the stallion, took Bones's hand, and laid it between the eyes of the stallion. "Here's a friend, Careless," he said, "be good to him. Take it easy and give him a chance."

Still holding Bones's hand, he sleeked the neck of the horse with it. The ears of Careless flicked forward but flattened against his skull again, giving his fine head an ominously snaky look.

"That's about all I can do for you, partner," Sleeper said. "Try him now."

The puzzled eyes of Bones dwelt for an instant on the face of his companion. "It's worse than hell for you to give him up, ain't it?" he asked. "Well, if I can manage it, he'll come back to you, when I'm through the pinch."

"Thanks," responded Sleeper. He stood at the head of the stallion, his hand against the muzzle of the great horse until Bones had mounted. Then he stepped back.

Careless rose from the earth like a disembodied flag of fire. Like the tossing of flame, he began to soar and smite the ground, and soar again. He went over backward. Bones, flinging himself clear, barely managed to leap into the saddle again as Careless sprang up. But he was not yet settled in the stirrups, when the stallion began to spin. Vainly Bones tried to right himself in the saddle. His body sloped more and more out to the side. He would certainly have been hurled like a stone from a sling if the voice of the master had not shouted suddenly. At that, Careless came to a snorting, stamping halt, throwing up his head, shuddering his skin in a vast desire to shake this unwanted burden from his back.

Bones slipped at once to the ground. "No good," he admitted. "There's more tricks in that big, silky devil than there is in any tinhorn's deck. How did you teach him this stuff?"

"I used to tie a sack of dirt on his back . . . tie it with twine . . . and then make him do the tricks to throw it off. Besides that, he knows some stuff of his own. I'm afraid that I've taught him too well."

Bones went to his mustang and mounted. "Come along with me," he said. "Talking won't make the miles any longer that lie ahead of this mustang."

They climbed to the higher ground, and, jogging toward the hills, Bones picked out the mouth of a ravine.

"D'you want to go down that valley?" Sleeper asked curiously. "I wouldn't, if I were you."

"Why not?"

"You'll be bottled up inside it."

"It's the quickest way through the hills . . . unless the gents have come out of White Water and started hunting for me. I dunno how they could've got word, though. It's a long ways off from where I had my trouble. But how did you know about me?"

"About what?"

"You knew there was a sheriff after me. Who told you that?"

"Sheriffs usually head up a manhunt."

"Well, but you talked about dead men. About two dead men."

"There wouldn't be one man. Anybody that knew you well enough to risk a gunfight with you would want to have a partner. If there were more than two, you'd probably get out of the way. If there were two, you'd likely fight it out. And if you fought, you'd be likely to kill. Still, it's just mostly guessing, about the two men."

"Kid, can I talk to you?"

"I'll tell you this," said Sleeper. "Any trouble you get from now on, is my trouble, too."

A sneer began to form on the face of the other, but it disappeared at once. "I've always been ready to play any hand against the world, Sleeper," he said. "But you're different, I can see that. A fellow that chucks away his chances and stays with his horse is a lot different from the rest of the world. All the way through you're different. But how did you know about the price on me?"

Sleeper looked at him and smiled. "Once I took a trail herd to Denver," he said. "After I played the town, I struck one place that had a hawk and an eagle . . . caged, they were. They had the same look in their eye that you have. They'd only been caught for a couple of weeks. . . . You've raised quite a lot of hell in your time, Bones."

Bones squinted at the distant horizon, and then sighed. "Yeah, I've raised my share of hell and now it's ready to burn me," he said. "But I've never been a killer, Sleeper. McGregor and Loftus, they needed a leadin' bad, and they got it."

"As how?" asked Sleeper.

"They did the grubstaking. I located the mine. They knew who I was. They knew that I was going straight . . . that I *had* gone straight for years. And they said that the past didn't matter with them, that they'd trust me, so I staked a claim. Free gold in quartz . . . the prettiest stuff you ever seen. They went out and had a look, McGregor and Loftus did, then they tried to make a big double-cross. If they turned me over to the law, I'd be lost, they'd get the mine, and I'd never see my half of it. You see? They jumped me in the middle of the night, with guns. But I had the luck. I left them both, and I left them dead. But now I'm on the trail again, and God knows where it'll end. That's my story, kid."

"It's a true story," said Sleeper. "You're sure you want to ride down this old bottle-necked ravine?"

"It's the short cut, Sleeper. Nobody around these parts is likely to know the law is after me with a price on my head. You only guessed it."

"Well . . . maybe it's the short cut, but I don't like it," answered Sleeper.

"Because you can afford to take the long way around . . . you with a horse under you that's as good as a pair of wings. But I've got to save miles. Pardner, they've put ten thousand dollars on my head!"

Sleeper translated the money into different terms, saying aloud: "Suppose that a 'puncher works like the devil and saves twenty a month. Four years to a thousand. Forty years to ten thousand. Why, the price on you is as much as a cowboy could save in a whole lifetime. And the hills are going to be full of men looking for you, Bones."

"All right. Let 'em try to find me!" snapped Bones.

III

"FOR A PARDNER"

They entered the mouth of the long ravine. It wound back into the hills, with the walls rising higher and higher and more precipitous every moment. Here and there were narrow cutbacks into the hills, but often, for a mile at a time, there was no chance to dodge to the right or to the left.

Bones, loosening the rifle in its saddle holster, occasionally looked up anxiously to the walls of the ravine, and then set his jaw the harder.

"Luck," he said. "There ain't anything but luck that a gent like me can pray for. Luck, and a good horse, and a gun that won't miss."

"You know what Sam Wu would advise you to do?"

"That Chinaman who teaches you the wrestling? What would he tell me to do?"

"Empty your guns, or throw them away."

"And give away my last chance?"

"He'd say that a chance to kill is not a chance worth having."

"Are you nutty, Sleeper? D'you believe what you're saying?"

"I try to believe it," said Sleeper. "Sam Wu . . . he's the one who keeps me from . . . well, he keeps me from being foolish a good many times."

"Listen!" exclaimed Bones. He lifted a quick hand. "You hear it?" he asked.

"No, what is it?"

"Listen . . . now you can hear it. A horse coming this way, fast."

Sleeper could finally make out the distant beating of the hoofs over the rocks and the earth, now clear, now muffled. Then, suddenly, around the next bend of the ravine came a rider full tilt, the horse swaying to a slant as it took the turn at full speed. In a moment the stranger was waving a hand high in the air.

Big Bones pulled in his horse with a grunt. "A friend," he said. "I didn't know that I had any friends up here."

The rider came on very fast toward the halted pair.

"Bad news," muttered Bones. "Good news would never come as fast as all of that."

"It's a girl!" exclaimed Sleeper.

She was dressed like a man from sombrero to boots; she was as slim and straight as a boy, too. But the touch of the wind showed a body softer than that of a man, and, as the brim of the sombrero flared up in the wind of the gallop, Sleeper could see the small face and the brightness of it.

She came up with a shout and a whoop, and skidded her pinto to a halt. "Hello, Bones!" she called, stretching out her hand.

"Hello, Maisry," he answered. "Dog-gone your blue eyes, but I'm glad to see you. What you doin' up here?"

"Who's that?" snapped the girl, looking straight with those blue eyes at Sleeper.

He saw the sleek of her black hair beneath her hat. She was dark as an Indian, almost. In fact, with that black hair she might have been an Indian, indeed, but the blue of the eyes told a different story.

"Calls himself Sleeper," Bones responded. "He's on the inside with me. What's the bad news?"

"Bad as hell," said the girl. "I hit White Water with the Colonel, and. . . ."

"The Colonel up here, too?" cried Bones.

"Be still while I tell you. You've got to hump, Bones. The first thing we ran into was news about you. They say that both McGregor and Loftus are dead. And you did it."

"Sure," Bones said calmly.

"I knew that hell would bust out of you," said the girl. "This *hombre* is all right, is he?" She jerked her head toward Sleeper.

"Sure. He's inside. How could that news hit White Water?"

"They pushed a relay through . . . rode night and day. The whole dog-gone town is cut loose into the hills. They knew that you're headed this way. They know that you're worth ten thousand dollars, dead or alive. Bones, what a wooden head you were to knock over McGregor and Loftus! You've got to turn back."

Bones looked over his shoulder. "If I turn back into the flat country, I'll run straight into the bunch that's coming up from the south," he said.

"We'll cut aside," said Sleeper. "They think you're headed north. We'll cut straight to the east. And ride like the devil."

"That's sense," said the girl. "There's a cutback we can ride through."

Sleeper nodded grimly. "Come on, Bones." He led with the stallion. They entered the narrow jaws of the cutback, and the horses began to struggle up the steep of the slope.

"When we get out, we'll be able to see something around us," said Sleeper, "but now we're in the wolf's throat."

"Got a nice kind of a way of putting things," remarked the girl. "The Colonel took the other valley and came south to warn you. Get the spurs into that fuzz-tail, Bones. You always rode horses that were only crow bait."

They began to rise out of the cutback. Soon they came up among the big boulders at the head of the little valley into sudden view of half a dozen men with leveled guns.

There was nothing to be done. Even Bones, to whom the moment meant the most, did not reach for a weapon. Of course, the hands of Sleeper were empty. It was only the girl who snatched out a .45 and said, with a wild flash of her blue eyes: "Shall we try 'em, Bones?"

"Back up, honey," answered Bones. "This game is over, and they're raking in table stakes."

Sleeper saw big Bill Collins, the sheriff, stand up from behind a small boulder and come slowly forward, stepping softly to keep his gun from being jarred out of line.

"Stick 'em up, Bones," he said. "I'll be damned if I ever thought that I could turn you into such easy money."

Bones raised his arms straight into the air and held them rigid there. "Sure it's easy money," he said. "Kind of tastes like blood, though, doesn't it?"

There was a perfectly simple explanation. From the high verge of the ravine, Sheriff Bill Collins and his men from White Water had seen the riders in the valley beneath, and, when the three bolted suddenly for the cutback, it was easy for the posse men to interpose.

"Kind of a small world!" was the way the sheriff put it. It meant five thousand dollars in head money to him, and a thousand apiece for each of his men.

"What about this other one . . . Sleeper?" asked one of the men. "What does he do in this game?"

"I dunno," said the sheriff. "I've always aimed to guess that he'd be in trouble, one of these days. A saddlebum that never does a lick of work is sure to get into bad company, sooner or later. Here he is with Bones. Who's the girl, Bones?"

"Ask her."

"What's your name?" asked the sheriff.

Her lip curled as she watched the broad, heavy face of Collins. "Maisry is my name," she said.

"Where d'you come from?"

"From Smith County."

"Smith County? Where's that?"

"Over yonder," she said, waving toward half the horizon.

"She's hoorawing you, Bill," said one of the men.

"It looked like to me," said the sheriff, as his men bound Bones's hands behind his back, "that you was pullin' out a

95

gun and aiming to make trouble, Miss Maisry."

"How did I know who you were?" asked the girl. "I didn't see your badge. I only saw your mug, and I thought you and the rest were a lot of rustlers."

"Rustlers?" shouted the indignant sheriff.

"Rustlers don't have time to wash, either," she answered, and reined her horse away.

"Bones, I'll be thinking about you," said Sleeper. He rode up on the stallion, holding out his hand.

"Keep back!" snorted Collins.

"Can't I say good bye to a friend?" asked Sleeper.

"None of your damned monkeyshines, or I'll have you in jail alongside of him. Get your horses, boys. This is a damned lucky day . . . I told you we'd get our man."

They started off, and Sleeper watched them go, his head fallen. Gradually the hoofs sounded far and faint.

"And what'll you do?" asked the girl.

"Find myself some grub," said Sleeper.

"Yeah. You look that kind," she answered savagely. "I thought that Bones was a friend of yours."

"He is."

"Ever do you a good turn?"

"Pulled me and the horse out of the creek, when we were drowning. That's all."

She looked curiously at him. "What are you, Sleeper?" she asked.

"A jail breaker, I guess," he answered gloomily. "Know anything about that business?"

She stared at him. "You mean for Bones?" she asked.

"Maybe. What are you, sister?"

"Oh, I just sashay around here and there," she answered. "But Bones has to be pulled out of jail."

"You know anything about McGregor and Loftus?"

"A pair of old double-crossing snakes. Tinhorns. Four-flushers. Killers. Why Bones ever threw in with them has me beat. The Colonel would have given him a hand when he wanted it."

"Bones was through with that breed," he said.

"That all you can say about the Colonel?"

"I never heard of him before, but he's a sort of a coyote, isn't he?"

"If you could ever get built up to the size of a real man," said the girl fiercely, "the Colonel would cut you down to a new size and then tell you something about himself."

"Well, so long," said Sleeper.

"You going?"

"You make me sort of tired," said Sleeper. "You've been around some tough *hombres,* and they've built you up a lot."

"They've what?"

"They've listened to your chatter. It's a funny thing, and a sad thing, too, what listening to a woman will do to her."

"What does it do to her?" she asked, coldly calm.

"What too much liquor does to a man," he replied.

"You wouldn't listen to a woman, would you?"

"Only in spots," he said.

"What spots?"

"Supper time, and other eating spots," said Sleeper.

"I'd like to do something about you, brother," said the girl.

"Get your men together and send them to call, someday," he told her. "So long."

"I hate to waste time on you," said Maisry. "But I'd like to know one thing. You really aim to try to help Bones?"

"I'm going to get him out of the jail, if that's what you mean. Or away from the rope, to put it straighter."

Suddenly the scornful fire died out of her eyes. "I kind of

97

half believe that you're not talking all the way through your hat," she confessed. "Suppose that we go and see the Colonel. He'll want to help."

"Suppose we do," said Sleeper.

IV

"THE PRICE OF A MAN"

They found the Colonel after dark, at a little shack not far from White Water. Maisry, as the dimly lighted window of the cabin shone through the brush, whistled twice on a high, sharp note, then she led the way to the door of the house. When she knocked, it was suddenly opened, although no one appeared in the lighted rectangle.

"Well?" demanded a shrill voice that might have belonged to either a child, a man, or a woman.

"I'm here with an *hombre* I've picked up," said the girl. "Shall we come in?"

"Come in, Maisry," said the high, piping voice, "but I wish you'd stop usin' the whole countryside for a grab-bag. What you brought home this time?"

"Kind of a sassy *hombre* with a sassy way of talking," said the girl. "Come on in, Sleeper."

She led the way through the door, and, as Sleeper stepped after her, he found himself in a typical shanty, a sort of wooden tent rather than a house. What was left of a stove, painted red with rust, stood in a corner, propped elaborately from beneath. There was no table. The floor was packed earth. The chief furnishings were a lantern, a roll of blankets on a tumble-down bunk, and the trappings and saddle for a horse that hung from a peg on the wall. This was a dull background for one of the strangest men that Sleeper had ever seen.

Sleeper thought first of a sack on stilts, or a blue crane with a human face on top of the bunchy body—the Colonel was like that. His legs were too long. They did not leave stomach room but seemed to divide the man to the chest. His arms and shoulders were extremely long and thick, and his huge head was put down with nothing to speak of in the way of a neck. He had a broad, pale, soggy face, with drooping mustaches and old-fashioned side-whiskers that dripped away on either side. His jowls were fat, bluish pouches that set off the paleness of his eyes. He had the look, altogether, of a brooding beast that is digesting and meditating.

"Hello, Sleeper," he said in his high-pitched voice. "Why did you let Maisry get her hands on you? She'll pick you as clean as a bone and throw you over her shoulder."

"Are you making me out a thief?" asked Maisry carelessly.

"You steal better things than hard cash," answered the Colonel. "Sit down, everybody. There's a stool . . . and that chair might hold you, Maisry."

"I'm not staying long. You know that Bones is in jail?"

"I know it. He's nearly had his neck stretched already. The crowd started gathering and yapping. They meant business. It's a long time since they've had the fun of lynchin' anybody in White Water. They sure would've opened that jail and taken out Bones to hang him, but somebody got up and made them a speech and said that it was a shame to hang Bones before he had a chance to confess and name all his crimes and his crooked friends. That speech made the crowd hold off for a while."

"Did the fellow who made the speech have long legs and a set of damn' silly sideburns?" asked the girl.

The Colonel smiled faintly at her. "Maybe he did. I wasn't looking him in the face," he said. "What's all this about?"

"Sleeper says that Bones pulled him and his horse out of

the water, and now he's going to do something to set Bones free."

The Colonel shook his head. "We may get Bones off with life instead of a rope, but that's the best," he said. "They're going to move Bones from the jail tomorrow."

"Why not catch him on the road, then?"

"Because he'll have a half dozen men with him, the same men who haven't collected their rewards, yet. And they'll watch him the way a bunch of lobos watch a bogged-down dogie."

"Half a dozen can be rushed!" exclaimed the girl.

"They can," agreed the Colonel, "and ten men can be lost fighting to save one. Does that make any sense?" He snapped his long fingers. "Bones is gone," he declared. "They're going to take him straight across country to the place where a lot of fools are hankering to hang him."

"I'm sorry," said the girl, with a sigh. "I've always liked Bones. Is he a goner, sure?"

"A dead goner."

"We've got some news, anyway," said the girl to Sleeper. "There's no use bothering about Bones any more."

"No?" said Sleeper. "But I *have* to bother. So long. I'll get started."

"For what? Wait a minute, kid," said the Colonel. "You can't do anything about Bones. I've told you that."

"I've got to appeal the case to a higher authority," Sleeper stated. With a wave of the hand he was gone into the night.

Back through White Water, Sleeper traced that higher authority. He heard of his man at the saloon. On Careless, he followed the trail out of White Water to a shack as wretched as that in which the Colonel was housed, but he found this one unoccupied. He rode on to a farm house that stood close to the trail, and heard the shouting and laughing of children that burst from the building with more brilliance than the lamplight.

When he heard this, Sleeper smiled and rode closer, until he could see, through the windows of the dining room, a group of grown people and half a dozen children watching a tall man with a bald head and a bunch on his back taking articles out of a great canvas bag. Already he had scattered queer little toys and dolls over the table, and now, as he went on showing to the housewife pieces of blue and white patterned cloth, he continued a chatter that kept the children whooping with laughter. The wife, however, seemed to be exclaiming over the cheap prices of the peddler.

For a fellow who seemed to distribute so much pleasure, he had one of the ugliest faces in the world, a very long and downward face with a huge slit of a mouth and a perfectly bald head made him seem old. In fact, he could not have been more than in early middle age. Now and then, in the very midst of his tales and his jesting, he would dart a glance at the rancher or his wife, or even at one of the children, that was like the look of a hawk when it sees prey beneath.

At the hitching rack, Sleeper found three mules that carried packs, their heads hanging patiently as they waited to be relieved from the burdens. When he spotted these poor freighters, Sleeper dismounted from the stallion and waited, hunkering on his heels in the shadows.

He did not have to stay there long. The door of the house opened, the peddler appeared with his sack on his back, the door letting out a gust of voices after him. The closing of the door shut out all light, and the peddler's footsteps came closer to where Sleeper crouched near the hitching rack. There the man opened one of the panniers that hung at the sides of a mule and put his hand inside it, muttering.

Sleeper remained motionless.

This muttering of the peddler broke off suddenly. His voice came in a low jarring note: "Who's there?" At last he had seen the dim outline of the horse against the bushes.

"Hello, Pop," answered Sleeper.

"Sleeper, eh?" exclaimed Pop Lowry. "You never was up this late at night . . . except for deviltry. What you up to now, eh?"

"Looking for a man," Sleeper explained.

"What kinda man, eh?"

"A gent who rides mules around the mountains, selling stuff for less than he paid for it. A gent who keeps in touch with high-graders bad as himself and uses them on jobs that he plans. A gent who's at the bottom of more trouble than all the rest of the cow thieves and bandits inside a thousand miles from White Water."

"I dunno who you mean, Sleeper."

"Sure you don't know. It would pain you a lot if you did."

"We're too close to the house," said Pop Lowry. "Let's get out on the road. Then we can talk."

He walked down the lane with the mules trudging after him, and Sleeper again on the back of the stallion. When they were in the road, Pop Lowry asked: "What's brought you to me, Sleeper? More trouble, I bet."

"Sure, it's trouble."

"I knew it," said Pop Lowry. "It's a kind of a sad thing the way that people bring their troubles to old Pop Lowry."

"You damn' old hypocrite!" exclaimed Sleeper.

"Steady, kid. Don't damn a man that you're going to try to use. You're raisin' my price when you talk like that."

"How d'you know that I'm going to use you?"

"I've got a sort of a chill up the middle of the spine, and I always know what that means."

"Pop, a fellow called Bones is in the jail. He's a friend of mine."

"They'll hang him sure." The peddler clucked softly. "A fine, high-spirited, young fool like you will want to help him out of his troubles. But you can't, Sleeper. I ain't one of those that look down on you. I've had a chance to guess at the stuff that's in you, even if you don't work with your hands. But you can't help Bones. He's a goner, sure."

"Maybe I can't help him, but you can."

"Me! A poor old man like me? You got some funny notions about me, Sleeper. You seem to think that. . . ."

"Can't we talk in the open?" asked Sleeper. "I know what you are, Pop. I'm the only man in this part of the world that even guesses. But in spite of what I know, I've held my tongue, haven't I?"

"The main reason that I got such a respect for you, son, is the way you don't go chattering," declared Pop Lowry warmly.

"Bones. I want him free. And with you helping, it can be done. There's mighty little that you can't change, if you put your mind to it."

The peddler chuckled. "A poor old man like me, hobblin' around the roads, workin' like a dog, winter and summer, what do you think I could do to turn Bones free? They're gonna watch him like wolves till they get their blood money."

"Talk sense, Pop," said Sleeper.

"There ain't any terms. There's ten thousand on the head of Bones. Well, gimme thirty thousand and I'll try what I can do."

"I haven't that much. I haven't any money at all."

"Why d'you waste my time, then?"

"I'll give you something else that you might turn into money . . . my time."

"*Your* time? My God, Sleeper, you drunk?"

"There are things you want done. I'll do 'em. And you'll help me to get Bones out of jail. I'll sell myself to do anything you want me to do."

"Hey . . . hold on! Lemme think about that. You'd sell yourself to me?"

"Just that."

"For life, eh?"

"For three months, say."

"Three months? Thirty thousand dollars is my price for helping Bones . . . it's a damn' mean job . . . the sort of a job I hate. And so you think your time is worth ten thousand a month, eh? What d'you think that I could do with you?" snarled the peddler.

"I'm not guessing at that. I don't want to guess. You'll send me to hell and back twice a week, I suppose. But I'll do anything, if you manage to help Bones."

"Anything?"

"Yes, I said that."

"I do a job worth thirty thousand. Instead of coin, I take the time of a worthless lazy kid for three months. What sort of a fool do you think that I am, Sleeper? Besides, how would I know that you'd keep your promise?"

"That wouldn't worry you. You know that I keep my word."

The peddler, after a moment, scratched a match and hollowed his hands to throw the light on Sleeper. He quietly endured the shining of the flame. The two big, grimy hands of Lowry looked like lifeless things, the protesting fingers of a copper statue.

"Well, I'll shake hands on it," said the peddler suddenly. And dropping the match, he held out his hand.

It was Sleeper's turn to pause, but, remembering how the

rope of poor Bones had pulled him and Careless from the water that day, he caught the hand of Lowry and shook it with a firm grip.

"They're taking Bones away from the jail tomorrow. You better get busy, Pop."

"Tomorrow? Too fast! Too fast! I got no time!" groaned Lowry.

"Start now," urged Sleeper.

"All right, then. You take the mules. Go back through the woods and camp where you find water."

"How'll you be able to find us later on?"

"I could find you the way a bloodhound follers a trail," said Lowry. "Because it's blood that I'll be hunting."

V
"A GIRL'S FAITH"

Back up the side of the mountains, sheltered by a grove of trees, Sleeper slept out the rest of that night after he had stripped the packs from the mules and the saddle from Careless. He slept into the warmth of the morning before Pop Lowry came striding through the trees, stepping big in his cowhide boots.

Sleeper built a cigarette, lighted it, and folded one arm behind his head. "How's things, Pop?" he asked.

Lowry sat down beside him. "Chuck this damned idea," said Lowry. "You can't get Bones free unless hell is raised."

"Raise it, then."

"I tell you, it's a mean job, Sleeper."

"Be mean, then, Pop. Bones has got to be saved."

"You ain't reasonable," said Lowry. "But if you *was* reasonable, you wouldn't be worth a damn to me!" He added, after a moment: "I'll stop the bunch who will ride with Bones at a place I'll tell you about. And I'll give you the key to the irons on his hands and feet. Is that worth three months of your time?"

"How many helpers do you give me?" asked Sleeper.

"Not a one. A crowd can't do the trick. One gent might wangle it, if he's slippery like you are. All a crowd could do would be to make a noise and kill off the bunch of guards. For killing them off I'd want more than three months of your time, Sleeper. I'd want more than all your time, maybe."

Sleeper considered. "All you do is to stop the people who've got Bones with them. And you give me the key to his irons. That's not so much, Pop. No friends at all for me to work with?"

"One man who won't see you, if you sneak up on them."

"One man who'll keep his eyes closed, eh?"

"Yes," said Pop. "Little fellow with long hair."

Sleeper, drawing out the long hunting knife, began to play with it as was his habit when his mind was occupied. Pop Lowry, fascinated, watched the knife wheel in the air and descend, always caught by the deadly point on the ball of Sleeper's thumb. It was like seeing a snake caught by the fangs as it lunged.

He kept lifting his glance from the flash of the knife to Sleeper's brooding eyes. Finally he said: "You're a queer one, Sleeper. I'd rather have poison poured into my coffee than you on my trail."

Sleeper said nothing. At last, slipping the knife away, he remarked: "It's the best that I can do. What's the look of the man who'll close his eyes when I come up?"

"You make the bargain?"

"I make the bargain. Three months of my time against this."

The eyes of the peddler flashed, and he held out his hand. "Shake on it, kid, and then I'll talk."

"Wash your hand before you offer it to me," Sleeper said evenly. "I've given you my word, and that's enough."

The peddler looked curiously down at his hand and then up at Sleeper's cold face. "You hate me a good deal, kid, don't you?" he asked.

"More than anyone else I know," answered Sleeper.

"Kind of a funny damned thing that we gotta throw in together, ain't it?" asked Pop Lowry.

"Call it that," said Sleeper. "Slip me the key and tell me where I'm to expect the guards."

"Here," said Lowry. He took out a flat-headed key and passed it over. "The same key fits the leg shackles and the handcuffs. And the place you'll find them will be over on the Thomas Flats. You know where the old draw runs across the Thomas Trail?"

"I know. There's a ravine down there with a lot of scrub growing in the bottom."

"That's it. It makes a pretty good camping place, with some water that's good enough for cattle and does for humans, too. That's where they'll stop tonight."

Sleeper's eyes narrowed thoughtfully. "How can you put on the brakes to stop them just there?"

"A couple of horses are gonna go lame, it appears," Lowry explained. He grunted, and his long, yellow teeth flashed like the teeth of a dog.

Sleeper nodded. "All right. Run along and let me sleep, then."

Lowry stood up, stretched himself, and looked down with interest at Sleeper. "If they don't get your scalp," he said, "I'm gonna use you to whittle out a lot of funny shapes of things. So long, kid. I'm glad that Bones has a friend, and I'm glad that the friend needed old Pop." He laughed, waved a hand, and went off to repack the mules.

Afterward, from the misty distance of sleep, a voice cut into Sleeper's drowsing. "I'll be out at the old shack. You know where . . . near White Water. You report there if you get Bones loose from trouble. So long, kid."

He was gone. One of the mules brayed far away, and, as this trumpet died out, silence fell around Sleeper. The copper bright stallion commenced to graze closer to him, lifting his head now and then to mark a change of scents on the wind, or a stir of shadows beneath the trees. . . .

It was already deep afternoon when he looked at the sun to gauge the time, washed at the water hole, dressed, and mounted the stallion. Sleep had rubbed a soothing hand right across the brow of care. He was ready for anything now, and he began to sing as he took the way down the slope and through the town of White Water.

A girl on a swift-moving gray mare rounded a corner and galloped past him, the sun bright in her hair. As she saw Sleeper, she pulled her mare around and came up beside him. The horse had cost money, and so had the girl. Her tan riding clothes had a special softness of texture that was like a dollar sign to the eye, and the silver on her hand-tooled bridle was the finest Mexican work, delicate beyond thought.

"Hey, Sleeper!" she called.

"Hey, Kate," he said, and pulled off his battered hat.

Her eyes were shining. He took a fresh pleasure in finding them brown. From a distance, she looked like one of those blue and golden beauties. The quiet brown of her eyes was always a surprise.

"Sleeper," she said, "you haven't been near me for days. Why don't you drift out to the house now and then?"

"I'm a little afraid of your father, Kate."

"Why, Sleeper, he says that you're one of the great people,

really. You don't have to be afraid of him any longer."

"All right. I'll try not to be."

"What's become of all your money? You're in rags again."

"You see, I ran into a faro game and felt lucky. But I was wrong."

"You'll be betting the hide of Careless, one of these days."

He sleeked the neck of the great horse, and Careless turned his head with a softening eye. "No, I won't bet Careless," he said quietly.

"But Sleeper, when are you going to grow up?"

There was a good deal of meaning behind that inquiry. He looked down at the sun-brightened dust and saw the shadows of the legs of the horses stenciled in black across it.

"I'm trying to get older," he answered. "Maybe time will help me."

"You ought to start work . . . steady work, Sleeper," she insisted. "Father will give you a place. Not just daubing ropes on cattle, but something with a future in it."

"Would he?" repeated Sleeper. His eye grew clear and bright. "I'm going to do it, one day," he answered. "I've got my hands full for a month or two, just now. And after that . . . I'm going to turn over a new leaf."

"Do you mean it, Sleeper?"

"I do mean it," he said grimly.

"Old Sleeper," said the girl, half sadly, half smiling. "You always have the right intentions but they don't grow very fast, do they? Where are you bound for now?"

"Oh, I'm bound out."

"It's always the out trail for you," sighed the girl. "Give me your hand, Sleeper."

He gave her his hand. She stripped off her riding glove before she took it, like a man.

"You'll come home and remember me, Sleeper?"

"Remember you? There's never a minute that I'm not thinking of you!" he exclaimed.

"Good bye, my dear," said the girl.

She turned her horse back down the street, and he rode the stallion from White Water into the open. Great resolutions were sweeping up into his mind as mountains sweep upon the eye.

There was no one else like Kate Williams, with the delicacy of a woman and the courage of a man. As soon as he had finished this business and the work of Pop Lowry, he would come back to her. He would settle down. He would get a job. And even when the days seemed endless and the course of the year one long agony, he would cling to his duty. That sort of thing, he ruminated, must be the common law of man. And if a fellow tries to escape it, his life is ruined, together with all the lives of the people around him. But he, Sleeper, no longer would waste his life, whittling in the sun.

He would show people that he was capable of continued effort. He might go to the legislature or something, in the end. He would be called an example for youth. And in the meantime, he would marry Kate Williams. Never take a penny of her father's money, but live in a hard-working poverty, honorable and industrious, a clean, meager, hard life.

He had reached such a point in his reflections that his breath was coming shorter and his breast heaving higher, and there was a thin measure of self-pity and desperate resolve in his eyes, also. But at this moment, a shadow moved through the brush at his right, and out flashed a lively pinto mustang ridden by Maisry. She waved her hand and called to him as she came up.

"Hello, Sleeper. Want some company?" she demanded.

Seen from a distance, she looked like a beautiful Indian

girl. Seen at close hand, the blue of her eyes was a shock of surprise and delight. He saw her, now, at close hand, and he felt the fullness of that shock.

"Company to where?" he asked.

"To Thomas Point," she answered.

"Who've you been talking to?" he demanded.

"You know. Old Pop Lowry. He seemed to have some ideas." She winked, and then laughed.

"What's your last name, Maisry?" he asked.

"Maisry Fellows is what I'm called."

"Maisry Fellows, will you do something for me?"

"That's what I'm here for," she replied.

"Then go home and stay there."

She frowned at him. "What home?" she asked.

"Any home. But start moving, will you?"

"Don't be so big and mean," answered the girl. "You know what you're up against, and an extra pair of hands may do you a lot of good."

He stared at her. When she was angry, a glow came over her. "What's a big tramp like Bones mean to you?"

"He taught me how to shoot."

"You're good, are you?"

"This good," she said.

A thin shadow trailed over them. As the girl lifted her head, Sleeper looked up and saw a hawk swinging low toward the ground, turning its pointed, evil head from side to side. The next moment a gun barked, and the hawk toppled from its place as though from the edge of an invisible cliff. It hit the ground hard, not twenty feet away.

"That's pretty good shooting . . . with a pop-gun," he remarked, noting her .32.

"Let me have your Forty-Five, then, and I'll show you," she declared.

"I haven't got a gun,"

"You haven't . . . what?"

"I haven't a gun."

"Wait a minute. I thought you were going to. . . ."

"I don't use guns. They weigh too much," explained Sleeper.

She stared in her turn, struck pale with astonishment. "You mean you're going to tackle . . . ?"

"You run along home and stop asking questions. Pop had no business talking to you, anyway."

"Sleeper, are you clean loco? They'll eat you alive."

"This comes of Pop talking to females!" he growled.

"Pop Lowry knew that you needed somebody to take care of you," said the girl. "And I'm going every inch of the way."

VI

"OWLHOOTERS' SHOWDOWN"

Dusk poured the draw full of a blue silvery haze, still there was some light from the horizon over the flats, but in the draw the fire of the camp gleamed like a searching eye. They were down under the high edge of the draw as Sleeper said to the girl: "You stay here and keep the horses for me."

"We'll tie the horses. I'm going on with you."

"You take my orders and obey them!" He could feel rather than see the anger in her eyes.

"I'd like to hit you, Sleeper," she said through her teeth.

"My God, you're pretty!" exclaimed Sleeper illogically, and he took her in his arms and kissed her.

Where was the ghost of Kate Williams, then?

"Let me go!" said the girl. "Except for making a racket and giving the show away, I'd make some trouble for this, you sneaking coyote."

"You're beautiful," Sleeper said, and kissed her again. Then he stepped back from her. "I'm sorry," he said.

"Do I go on with you now?" she pleaded, quite overlooking his actions.

"You stay back here with the horses."

Maisry groaned but did not argue, so Sleeper left her and commenced stalking the camp. What had Lowry meant by talking? Above all, what had he meant by talking to a girl?

Sleeper came through the lower ring of trees. Between him and the campfire was the level surface of the water hole. The flame painted it with long orange streamers, dazzling bright except when one of the moving shadows near the fire walked across its light and killed the reflection. There were seven men in the camp, and one of them was Bones, of course. At a little distance from the men, the horses were hobbled to graze in the tall, rich grass. In the shaking of the firelight, they looked like nameless monsters.

Sleeper slipped back inside the brush and moved around the expanse of the water until the firelight shone strongly at him through the trees. Then he went forward on hands and knees. He could hear the voices inside the camp clearly.

Sheriff Bill Collins was posting a guard to walk up and down in the brush or along the edge of it. His speech was one of interest.

"We got a ten thousand dollar package of goods along with us. A thing that's worth that is worth the stealing. If he's worth ten thousand to the law, he's worth a pile more to his friend, maybe. We've got to keep our eyes open. Three of us will walk guard for three hours. Then the next three for the next three hours. And after that, we'll make our start. Understand? You boys step out here and keep your eyes open. Look mighty sharp. If you see anything stir, shoot first and holler second."

113

The guard was instantly posted. As they began to walk up and down, Sleeper shrank flat in a patch of tall grass fenced on either side by small shrubs. The path of one of the guards passed within a few steps of him, and he had to make himself small.

He could see that there was little chance to withdraw, and no chance at all of making an approach closer to the fire until the guards were changed. That meant three hours of lying on the cold, damp ground. If he fell asleep, he might snore, so he'd have to stay awake. By a great effort of will Sleeper worked the nervous tremors out of his arms and legs and lay very still. The cold from the ground seemed to soak up through him as though his body were porous.

And so the time wore by like a snail, hour after hour of the monotonous silence.

There was little talk at the campfire. Bones sat up, making a slight jangling of his chains whenever he moved. Once Collins said: "How does it feel to be worth ten thousand dollars, Bones?"

Bones answered: "Ask me how it feels to be dead, will you? I ain't gonna see any of the money I'm sold for." After that, Bones lay down, and the sheriff followed.

The little man with the long hair was not by the fire. He was the one of the three guards who moved up and down on the farther side of the camp, and now and then it was he who came in and put fresh fuel on the flames. As he did this, on two occasions, he stood up and looked earnestly around him. That attitude of his had a definite meaning for Sleeper. The man was expecting something.

Something rustled in the grass behind Sleeper. He started as a body slid to rest beside him and the whisper of Maisry Fellows said: "I couldn't wait it out any longer, Sleeper. Sorry."

"You three-ply idiot," murmured Sleeper in answer. "Back out of this."

"I can't without being noticed," whispered the girl. "Look at that damn' moon coming up to spoil everything."

The moon appeared as a flaming pyramid in the east, a pyramid that brightened by degrees and waxed, until the wide, yellow rim of the moon appeared. It increased, clung for a moment by the lower rim, like a bubble stuck to a glass edge. Then it was detached and floated softly up the sky, shrinking a little, growing less yellow, casting every moment a brighter and a whiter light.

No sun, it seemed to Sleeper, ever had shone with such deadly force. The flat of the bottomland was streaked with intense shadows overlaid upon clear silver. And how could the eyes of the guards fail to find two figures that lay only half hidden behind the brush and in the grass?

"It's great, isn't it?" whispered the girl.

"Grand," said Sleeper sourly. "Helpful as hell to us, right now."

"Are you afraid?"

"Yeah . . . plenty. How about you?"

"Frightened silly . . . and I love it."

He grinned a little as he heard this. It had the true honest tang to it. That other figure, that brown-eyed Kate, became rather dim in his mind. Black hair and blue eyes—that seemed the only proper color with which beauty should be stained.

The guard in front of him suddenly walked up to the fire and said: "Turn out, you fellows! Turn out! Our three hours are up!"

Sleeper was out of his place in the grass in an instant, gliding forward. He had spotted a patch of brush well inside the circle around which the guards marched. It was daring

115

danger to make this move, but at least he would be within reaching distance of the prisoner from there.

As he sank into the shrubbery, he felt a sudden relief, having taken a step from which there was no drawing back. But at that same moment, striking him as unexpectedly as a blow on the back, a sneeze exploded from his throat.

"What's that?" shouted the voice of Bill Collins. "There . . . in that bush?"

Sleeper had no gun. He had only his knife, and the cold handle of that was instantly in the grasp of his fingers when he heard the voice of the girl say, from behind him: "Well, does it throw a chill into all you gents to hear a girl sneeze?" She was walking calmly into the camp, covering up his telltale exploit with her presence.

"What's that?" two or three shouted.

"It's Maisry," Sheriff Collins announced. "What the devil are you doing here, Maisry Fellows? What are you up to?"

"Maisry, have you gone loco?" demanded the husky voice of Bones.

"I wanted to see you again, Bones," said the girl. "How are things?"

"Pretty fair. You're crazy to come down here this time of night."

"Just a lot of big brothers, all these *hombres*," said the girl. "And I like to travel in the cool of the night. Why not?"

"I thought that sneeze sounded nearer. I thought it sounded right out of that brush, there," insisted Bill Collins.

"I'll take a look," answered a voice. It was the little man with the long hair. He walked straight into the patch of shrubbery—and struck his foot against the body of the hidden man.

Sleeper, his arms drawn back with the knife, waited. He saw the convulsive start of the other, then he heard the little man of the long hair saying calmly enough: "Why, I dunno

116

what you heard, but it sure didn't come from here, unless this scrub oak an' blackjack can sneeze by itself."

"Is there something I can do for you?" asked Maisry of Bones. "I didn't have a chance to talk to you before they slammed you into the jail. You tell me what you want, and maybe I can get it for you, and send it along. You still have friends in the world. Don't you forget that, Bones."

"Thanks," said Bones. "I'll tell you what you can do for me, sister. Hike out of here, and hike fast."

"Where's your hoss?" asked the suspicious sheriff.

"Over there. I left him back a ways while I made sure that this was really the camp that I was looking for."

"Hoping you might sneak up and give Bones a hand, eh?" sneered Bill Collins. "Wouldn't it have been sweet if a smooth-faced brat like you had took Bones away from six growed-up men? I dunno why you done this, girl, but now git out of here and git fast. We don't wanna be bothered."

"Thanks, Sheriff," said the girl. "And so long, Bones. Sorry about everything."

Maisry walked away from the fire, slowly, and straight past the undergrowth where Sleeper lay. Passing it, her step slowed until it seemed that she was about to halt, but she mastered that impulse and went straight on into the taller shrubbery. The crackling of the branches ceased. She was gone.

In the meantime, the second guard had taken his post, with the sheriff among its members.

"The jails is too full of men," was Collins comment on this visit. "There had oughta be a little room left for the girls . . . sassy brats like that one." And he began to walk his beat, just behind the waiting form of Sleeper.

The relieved guards, well tired by their duties, were quickly wrapped up and asleep, all except the little man with

117

the long hair. He, on the contrary, seemed to have something in mind that kept him wide awake. It was thought for his horse, perhaps. For now he stood up and brought from the hobbled line of grazing animals a good, upstanding gelding, from the legs of which he took the sideline and the hobbles. He pulled a bridle over its head.

"What's the idea there?" demanded the sheriff.

"I'm kind of worried," said the little man. "Suppose something was to happen . . . suppose a gent, instead of a girl, showed up . . . well, there's not a hoss in the camp that's ready to be moved."

"That's good sense, too," Collins agreed. "That's more sense than you ever showed before, Pete."

Collins resumed his beat, while Pete turned and sat again by the fire, near the prone figure of Bones.

And right up into the shadow cast by Pete moved the flat, slithering body of Sleeper. He entered that long, slanting shadow from the fire, but still the moon shone on him with plenty of light. He could only hope that he might not be seen by any of the guards for the simple reason that they would not look for him there.

Now he was reaching to Bones, whispering: "Bones, it's Sleeper. Lie still. Don't stir. I've got the key."

The faint whisper of Bones answered in a hiss: "You damn' young fool, them buzzards will pick you clean an' leave your bones rotting here."

Sleeper found the handcuffs, scratched softly with the point of the key until he located the entrance slot, and in another moment Bones's wrists were free. He took the key in his own fingers and sat up.

"What's the matter there?" called the voice of the sheriff.

"I'm gonna smoke," answered Bones, and at the same time worked the key into his ankle irons.

Ahead of them, a low, guarded voice said: "Pretend to hit me over the head and knock me out. I'm leavin' my gun lyin' on the ground. . . ."

"The horse is right behind you, Bones," whispered Sleeper. "Grab it and jump on its back. Head straight across the bottom to the south. Straight across. I've got my horse there."

Bones nodded silently. "I'd like to salt away some of these guards with lead," he whispered a moment later.

There was a very soft clicking sound that told that his feet were free. "Now," said Sleeper. "On the run, Bones."

For his own part, he whirled to his feet as Bones arose. The sheriff, behind him, cursed and cried out: "Stop! Who's there?"

Sleeper struck Pete's head with the flat of his hand, and Pete keeled over as though he had been hit by a sledgehammer.

Bones's long, lanky body leaped for the horse.

"Wake up! Turn out! Hell's loose!" Collins yelled, and fired his rifle. He put one bullet somewhere through space. Then a streak of light left the right hand of Sleeper, as he threw the knife from the flat of his palm, whipping it across the tips of his fingers. It was a simple thing to do if one was born for it and had had twenty years' constant practice. The knife was not aimed at the breast of the sheriff, or he would have been a dead man on the spot. It was directed toward his right shoulder, and through the flesh of that shoulder it glided.

The lawman dropped his rifle with a yell and caught out the weapon that was buried in his flesh. Past him flashed the racing mustang with Bones riding bareback on it. Past him went the streaking form of Sleeper.

"Sleeper!" shouted Collins in a moment of recognition.

"It's that damn' kid . . . it's Sleeper . . . oh, damn your heart, you've ruined me! Horses! Horses! For God's sake get the horses! We've let ten thousand dollars slip through our fingers, you fools!"

Sleeper, hearing the voice, listened to the crackling of gunfire, heard the bullets rush through the branches about him. He had been recognized, and he knew what that meant—a life of stealth outside the law—a life of cold wandering, cast from the law-abiding society of men. He was an outlaw from this moment. And that word had always brought up into his mind the picture of a lone wolf, skulking, head down, through the white rage of a blizzard, hunching his gaunt belly against its backbone.

He had that picture and went blind with it. A moment later he slipped, struck against a tree, and fell back on the ground with his breath thoroughly knocked out of him. His brain was clear enough. It told him to get at once on his feet, and that he could not be defeated by such a silly chance at this time. He did in fact regain his feet, but he was doubled over, gasping, and his legs staggered, weak at the knees, when he tried to run. Like a man shot through the belly he struggled forward, biting at the air with his teeth, like that very picture of the wolf that he had conceived.

And behind him, the sound of galloping horses had begun! He gasped for breath. He could never get to the place where the girl had tethered the horses. They would sweep up on him and shoot him down. . . .

Instead, he stood still, drew in a desperate breath, and whistled a sharp, shrill note. Then he staggered forward again. Every muscle in his bruised chest and stomach was tensed hard as a board. Hoof beats swept toward him; he knew the long sweep and rhythm of them. Careless had heard the call and had broken away. He would have snapped strong ropes to answer that whistle.

Careless came, as Sleeper shouted with a gasping breath. The moonlight turned the beautiful horse to silver, to flowing, wet silver. Then he was beside his master. He was ready at hand, as Sleeper pulled himself up into the saddle. There were no reins for him to lift. They had been broken off close to the bits, but reins were hardly needed. A pressure of the knees or of the hand would guide Careless when his master was mounted on him.

The hard rushing of the hoofs, the shouting behind threatened like a wave to overwhelm them, but in another moment the stallion was off. And Sleeper left the confusion and the danger behind him as a rising bird leaves the ground. Through the last of the brush he galloped. The unbroken sweep of prairie showed, and the steep bank of the draw. He went up it like a springing goat up a mountainside. And on the level above appeared the girl and Bones—she with her rifle drawn from the saddle boot, ready to cover the retreat.

There was no need for rifle fire now. There was only need to follow the headlong pace of the stallion, if they could. Behind them, from the draw, came a wild outburst of yelling. It sounded to Sleeper like the baying of hounds.

The chase lasted only a short time. In the next draw they doubled back out of sight and sound of the manhunt. Before dawn they were in the high hills where they made a pause and looked out over the plains, still dark with the lower shades of night.

The trio had loosened the cinches of the horses. Sleeper and Bones stood on either side of the girl with their arms interlocked behind her. And she looked up to one face and then to the other in a fervor of enthusiasm.

"It was the greatest night of my life!" she cried. "It was

better than dancing with the King of England. It was wonderful, Bones! It was glorious! And, Sleeper, what a man you turned out to be!"

He smiled, not at the girl, but at the darkness of the wide world before him. That was how life seemed to him, and all the future—filled with danger.

Bones reached a hand across to him, and he gripped it silently. Sleeper then had a strange and perfect sense of duty fulfilled. He had embarked upon the out trail where he had to go, and it made no difference if the trail never turned back.

The Welding Quirt

"The Welding Quirt" first appeared in the April 12, 1924 issue of Street & Smith's *Western Story Magazine*. It was published under Faust's Max Brand pseudonym. Its storyline is very much the tale of the prodigal son played out in the Western setting of Wooster, and deals with the issue of character. The story has never before appeared in book form.

I

" 'SNOOZER STANDS ALONE' "

When it is said of one man by another that he has character, it usually means that he is grasping in his money affairs, or that he has buried in his heart a deep grudge against all of the world and a determination to injure all living things except himself. Because we respect force blindly, as an attribute of gods, we wrap all of these manifest brutalities in the muffling and digni-fying word: *character*.

The moment one laid eyes on the Mells, it was plain that they had character. The whole school knew that young Snoozer Mell had character—loads and chunks of it. It stuck out in him just as the topknot up above his skull. It showed in his pale blue, meditating eyes, in the rarity of his smiles. On the very first day, one of the older boys played a bit of a trick upon Snoozer in the schoolyard, and Snoozer said not a word until after three o'clock, when the whole rout of pupils was pouring homeward through the village. Then Snoozer cornered his man and cut him to pieces with calmly, well-directed fire. When, reeling and on his knees, and his two eyes swollen, the elder youth finally announced that he had enough, Snoozer stared down at him with cold, incalculable malice. Finally he raised his foot, placed the side of it carefully in the middle of the beaten boy's face, and pushed him over on his back.

After that, the whole town knew that Snoozer Mell had character. He had very few fights after this. The point was that he could never find anyone willing to stand up to him save when, now and again, a new boy came to town and entered the school—some long, strong, brown-faced youngster, made hardy by a man's work on the range long before he was out of boyish years. When such strangers arrived, the rest of the school stood back and allowed the foreigner to try the edge of his blade upon Snoozer. There was never other than one result. Snoozer was usually smaller. He would stand away at first, working his long arms and his wide, thick shoulders smoothly to keep the other at a distance. For five minutes he might play deftly around his antagonist. Then he would begin to make execution upon his foe with sudden, smashing blows. And when the end came, he would walk quietly away with that same still light in his pale blue eyes. Usually he would not have said a word during the encounter.

Snoozer had a father with just as much character as he. Snoozer's father was very opposite from his son in many ways. He had, for instance, a rough, sallow skin compared with Snoozer's delicate, white one. He had a short, thickly curled beard, and his face was made strange by a lofty forehead that swelled out at the top into a great bulge. He was an ugly man. His ugliest feature was a high-arched, enormous, crooked nose. He looked like an eagle at the first glance, like a devil at the second, and then like something else—no one could say exactly what.

What the town first discovered about Harrison J. Mell was that he was able to lift eleven hundred and fifty pounds of old iron junk in a sack. He actually did that in the Loomis blacksmith shop. The knowledge of that, combined with the early tales of his son's prowess in the school, made the whole village say: "Like father, like son. He's a chip off the old block!" Except that the boy was supposed to be much milder than his sire, and he was so much better looking.

However, it must not be supposed that the Mells did nothing but make trouble. As a matter of fact, they were very law-abiding citizens. The boy did his schoolwork and received excellent grades. After school he was observed working about his father's house, sawing stove wood, or taking care of the chickens, or milking the cow. In the summer months he would get out on the range and work at half pay, doing more than two men's work. That is generally the case with boys when they hire out. He had not been a single season in the village before it was known that the youth was an expert with a rope, that he could read a trail like an Indian, and that a bucking horse was his idea of being rocked to sleep.

Snoozer was valued at once, and every summer there was a scramble for his services. His father, in the meantime, had joined old Loomis in the blacksmith shop and finally worked into a full partnership, for the fame of his glorious strength of arm brought much trade to the place, and every little child in the village, sooner or later, would stand among the smoky shadows at the door of the smithy and watch the giant beating showers of sparks from the iron bars until their hearts failed them and they ran away to dream, for many nights, of great, sooty devils with small eyes and huge, crooked noses.

No one could recall that Harrison J. Mell ever did an un-
kind or wicked thing since he came to the village, but still no
one wished to meet his eye. As for trouble, he fell into it only
once. A huge-armed giant came into town and said that he
had heard about Wooster's strong man, and wanted to *talk*
privately with him. Half a hundred of Wooster's citizens es-
corted him at once to the Loomis shop. There they stood by
and saw Harrison J. Mell receive a blow upon the cheek, and
then they saw him pick the stranger from the ground and literally break him in the air, between his hands. He threw down
the bent, crippled body and went back to his forge, while the
citizens of Wooster carried the fallen one away.

After that, anyone in the town or from the surrounding
range would far rather have stood before a machine-gun than
before Harrison Mell. He became a thousand times more
marked than he had been before. When little boys saw the
strong man in the circus they would say: "My, ain't he strong!
He must be pretty near half as strong as Harry Mell!" That
fairly well expressed the attitude of the town toward their new
blacksmith.

Yet the prodigious strength, the remarkably ugly and cruel
face, and the lofty stature of Harrison J. Mell never produced
upon the town the same effect as that which was made by his
son when Snoozer went down the street with his springy step
and his head a little to one side. For, after all, the father could
be understood. He had the bulk that went with strength. But
Snoozer grew up to be hardly more than middle-size. And
among other men he was like the owl among birds, for he was
always silent. Snoozer was twelve when he came to town; he
was sixteen before Wooster decided that while he had character, his was a bad character—bad to the core.

This came about in the following manner. It was Halloween, and the youngsters of Wooster roamed abroad to hunt mischief and enjoy the trouble that they made. The others went out in groups of three and more. Snoozer went out by himself to look on. For he had no playmates, he never had had a real companion, and he would not try to find one on this night. When his chores were ended, supper finished, and he had washed the dishes, he left his father smoking a pipe and reading a paper in the front room while he slipped out into the night. He saw lighted pumpkin heads at the windows. He saw strange masks and stealthy-footed troops along the streets, and Snoozer went along in his soundless way, seeing everything and joining nothing until he came to the church.

There he found a group of half a dozen of the older youths engaged in hoisting the minister's buggy, wheel by wheel and bit by bit, to the top of the church steeple. In the midst of this pleasant occupation came the sheriff and two deputy sheriffs to rout the merrymakers and bring order out of chaos. All the others fled with delighted shouts, but Snoozer did not flee. He would not even hasten his pace as he walked away. He would not even turn his head to watch the pursuit, and so the hands of the sheriff's two deputies fell upon his shoulders at the same moment, and they jerked him about so violently that his hat fell off.

"We got one of 'em!" panted a captor to the sheriff. "One's enough. We'll make him climb up the steeple and lower them things down again!"

"It's young Mell," said the sheriff, flashing his lantern in the face of the blacksmith's son. "Might've knowed that he was at the bottom of this here hell-raisin'. Now, youngster, you shinny right up that steeple and start to work!"

But Snoozer did not budge.

"Quick!" said the sheriff. "March right on this way back

to the church, kid, and. . . ."

Here he made what was afterward admitted to be a false move, for he drew out a long Colt revolver and flourished it under the nose of Snoozer. As he later explained, it was not that he wanted to use it, but he expected to give the lad a fright that would last him the rest of his life. Snoozer, however, refused to be frightened. He merely twitched his long, muscular arms away from the keeping of the sheriff's men and smote the sheriff himself upon the root of the nose, and tumbled that dignitary down as though he had been a ninepin. One of the deputies picked up his chief. The other attempted to capture Snoozer and was knocked down for his pains, after which Snoozer walked deliberately home without hastening his pace.

There he was found by the irate trio.

"Where's Snoozer?" they asked of his father.

The father looked them over calmly. Then he raised the deep thunder of his voice: "Snoozer! Come here!"

"Better go get him!" suggested the sheriff. "He knows what's up, and he won't come himself."

"You don't know Snoozer," said his father.

And presently the boy appeared in the doorway, quite unaltered, with his head, as usual, cocked a little to one side. There was a growl of rage from the three, and they lurched at Snoozer. He did not retreat, but he brought from behind him an old-fashioned rifle, with a massive, octagonal barrel. He tossed it lightly across the crook of his left arm and put a finger on the trigger.

There was no need of a command. The three scattered as though a charge of birdshot had struck them.

"Gimme that gun," Harrison J. Mell ordered.

It was surrendered to him without a word, and the three would have closed on him again, but here Harrison Mell rose from his chair and commanded them to keep their distance until he knew what was wrong. They told him. It was breaking the peace, then riot, then resistance to arrest, then assault upon officers of the law. Quite a formidable charge, take it all in all.

"Did you do all them things?" asked Harrison.

There was silence.

"Did you hit the sheriff?"

"Yes," Snoozer answered.

"Take him, Sheriff," said the father sadly. "Take him and see that he gets everything that the law can give him. I been waitin' for a bad streak to come out in him. Maybe this is where it starts."

II
"NO GOOD FOR NOTHIN' "

The justice of the peace was a wise and kindly old man. He was familiar with both sides of crime. That is to say, he had been on the other side of the fence when he was a young man, and he had learned about the evils of the world of sin at first-hand. That knowledge, since it did not spoil him, left him at once mellow and hard. For, knowing how black are the shadows of vice, he hated it with all his heart—he hated it the more because he himself had once almost been drawn down into the slough.

When he looked down on the calm face and the thoughtful eyes of the boy, who was watching him steadily, unblinkingly in return, he said to himself: *If this youngster were afraid of me, I'd simply give him a fatherly lecture that would raise his hair on end. The trouble is that the young rascal hasn't a nerve in his body. He's as calm as though he were sitting down to the table.*

So he made a peroration that was eloquent enough to have been worth repeating to every bad boy in the world. He talked about the manner in which evil enters the mind. He talked about the way it grows and spreads like an evil weed or the germs of a disease. He told of the bitter and the stern measures that must be taken to repress weeds before they choke the garden. And having ended this peroration, he told young Snoozer that he would remain in jail for thirty days, and that, if there were another offense of this sort, he would receive a sentence thirty times as severe.

So it was that Snoozer went to jail. It gave him thirty days of physical confinement. And it gave him thirty days of silence during which he could develop his ideas about the world in general and about justice in particular.

Deep in his heart, first of all, was the conviction that he had been gravely injured. In the beginning he had been utterly innocent. He had not touched a hand to the hoisting of the buggy up the face of the steeple. Yet he had been attacked by the officers of the law, and still he had not resisted until a gun was flashed in his face. It seemed to him that if his innocence was not the snowiest white, then there was no such thing in the world as being without guilt. Being convinced of this, the more he brooded upon it the more his reflections fortified him. If he had been told that he was being sentenced not at all for taking part in a Halloween prank but for resisting arrest and actually assaulting officers of the law, he would have considered such a reflection ridiculous in the extreme.

Then his mind passed on to other matters. He considered that speech of his father at the very moment when he was being arrested. There had been an effort on the part of Harrison Mell to learn the story as his son might be able to tell it. He had accepted only one angle of the yarn and proceeded to judgment with only the fragment in his possession.

Of course, Snoozer might have pleaded his case both before his father and before the judge. But he disdained doing so. Being innocent, he would have scorned to plead his innocence in the face of others. It would be too much like begging for what was his due. And the boy's dignity, of which there is no greater and sterner emotion, prevented him.

He served out his thirty days and walked forth from the jail to the street.

His father should have been there to meet him and to escort him home, he felt. He should not be left to skulk along through back alleys until he reached the shelter of the familiar walls. At that, he drew himself up and vowed that he would *not* skulk. He would meet every eye that cared to fall upon him. Let no man dare to sneer or to point when Snoozer passed.

He had not walked a block before he met the justice of the peace himself, and that benevolent old gentleman hurried across the street to stop him.

"Snoozer," he said, "I've just discovered that you didn't have a share in that scurvy trick which the other boys played on the preacher. I can see, now, how you were drawn in and how you had a right to resist the officers of the law. If I had known this, I should have given you a reprimand only, and . . . I'm sorry, Snoozer, because. . . ."

His voice fell away, for there was not the slightest spark of kindliness in the blue eyes of Snoozer. With his head characteristically tilted a little to one side on his thick neck, he was staring passively up into the face of the old lawyer, judging him, reading him, despising him.

Scorn is something that we feel with a knife edge of pain even when it is only the scorn of a child. The kindly feelings of the judge withered instantly within him. He grew red of face, with a little pale spot of anger in the center of either cheek, and then he brushed on his way past Snoozer without another word. When he reached the courthouse, he found that he was panting, almost as though he had been running all the way.

"That boy," said the justice of the peace to himself, "is coming to a bad end."

So thought the rest of Wooster before nightfall, as they watched young Snoozer walking down the streets toward his home, going from the jail sentence with an eye as contented, a face as calm, a step as light and springy as ever.

"That boy will come to no good end!"

So thought Harrison J. Mell himself, for, when he came home from the blacksmith shop, he found his son seated in the front room with a small valise at his side, together with a blanket roll and his rifle.

"What's wrong now, Snoozer?" asked the smith. "Ain't you had your lesson? You goin' hell-raisin' ag'in?"

"I'm leavin' you," Snoozer said in his quiet way. "I guess you ain't goin' to care much, but I thought I'd wait till you come home, so's you could hear me say it."

"Leavin' me?" echoed the father with a gasp.

"Leavin' you," repeated Snoozer.

"How come?"

A hundred bitter reasons rushed into the mind of Snoozer. Tears of self-pity were stinging the roots of his eyes. But he winked them away and even managed that faintest of smiles which was his nearest signal of mirth or of good nature.

"I thought that I'd take a trip. Want to see things," Snoozer explained.

His father turned suddenly and looked out the window.

That's all he cares, whispered Snoozer to his soul, and rose stiffly from his place.

"The trouble is . . . ," said the father.

"Well?"

"The trouble is, Snoozer, that all the folks in this here

town of Wooster'll be sayin' that you run away because you was ashamed to stay and face 'em"

It was the fall of the whiplash, and Snoozer winced under it. There was a long silence, and then he said: "Well, if you don't mind havin' me around, I guess I'll stay a while."

His father said not a thing except: "Maybe you better stay a while."

And Snoozer walked haltingly from the room. With every step, he was burdened by the feeling that so half-hearted a welcome should make him deny his father's house at once and send him out to seek another home. And with every step, the hot words came up to his tongue. But he crowded them back.

He did not see his father drop into a chair and bury his face in his hands, for Snoozer was walking slowly up the stairs, like an old man. He went to his room. Something was flooding up in him, choking his throat, stinging his eyes. He hardly knew what it was. For he had been a man since he was eight years old, and there had been no time for womanish display of emotion in the last half of his life. Upon entering his room, he saw, hanging from its nail on the wall, the picture of his mother. All at once the knees of Snoozer sagged beneath him. He dropped beside the bed and began to sob. He fought against them with all his might, for if they were heard—if he were heard to weep!

Yet even the horror of that thought could not stop him. From the very pit and inmost deeps of his being those wild sobs were born and rose and shook him. He crawled to the window, and there, on his knees, he gasped in the cooler air until the passion of weakness left him. Then he was able to draw himself up to his feet, find a chair, and sink into it.

Most of all, he was bewildered, and he told himself bitterly that it could not be he who had fallen into this womanish weakness. It could not be Snoozer Mell. In the height of his self-scorn, he went to the mirror and studied his swollen, reddened, face. At least, God be praised, there had been no tears. Yet he dared not again look at that picture on the wall. He knew now what had unnerved him. It was the thought of his dead mother's voice that had fallen upon his heart like a soothing hand touching his head, as she had touched it in the old days.

He bathed his face in cold water until the redness was gone. Finally he could venture down the stairs. He had to pass through the room where his father was, but luckily Harrison Mell was closely masked by his newspaper, and so Snoozer reached the kitchen and set up a racket of pans, and rattled at the stove until he was breathing easily once more. Then: "What'll you be havin' for dinner, Dad?"

The deep voice of the father returned: "Don't you be botherin', Snoozer. I'll cook up something soon as I've rested a while."

Snoozer leaned against the sink, sick and weak. There could be no doubt. His father hated him now, and did not even wish to eat food that the hands of his son had prepared. But he made no answer. What answer could he make?

Eventually Harrison Mell came out, passed through the kitchen, and went into the back yard. Then came the sound of the hatchet falling. Snoozer glanced out the window, and his heart stood still, for there was his father chopping the kindling wood.

Oh, God, Snoozer whispered to his sad soul, *he don't think that I'm no good for nothin' no more.* Then he began to slice the bacon.

They ate supper in silence. For that matter, they usually were silent when they were together, but tonight a different quality, like speaking voices, had crept into the quiet. When the meal ended, Harrison Mell went out into the kitchen. He washed the dishes with his great, veined hands, while Snoozer wiped them, after which they returned to the living room. Harrison sat down to his paper, with his glasses perched on his huge, crooked nose. But what seemed odd to Snoozer was that Harrison Mell sat for a whole long hour reading with great intentness and yet without ever turning a page!

III

"KID DUFFY"

If either of them had been able to talk, all would have been well, but neither was a man who really turned thought into words. What Harrison Mell thought he was doing when he chopped the kindling and helped in the household work was showing his son that he realized the punishment of the latter had been greater than his crime. What Snoozer thought was that his father was now bluntly telling him how he was unnecessary in the household. And that atmosphere drove him out into the streets.

It should be remembered that Snoozer was only sixteen and not over large for his age. But his silence was that of a man. His reserve and poise would have given credit to a mature person. God had placed in his hands, already, the strength and the adroitness of a fully developed athlete. He would never grow heavier or taller than he now was. His muscle could only harden and grow more capable of handling heavy burdens. He was young in years, but old in experience.

Moreover, he was a jailbird. No one could overestimate what that fact meant in his life. If a stranger commented upon him as he roamed through the streets of the town with his peculiar, quick, soft footfall, someone was sure to answer: "That Snoozer Mell, he's a hard one. Only a kid, to look at him. But he beat up three law officers when they tried to arrest him. They come to his house. He sticks 'em up with a rifle. Well, he only got a month in jail. Pretty easy for him, I'd say."

A pleasant introduction for a youth of sixteen who had never broken the law with malice aforethought. It was through such words as these that he was presented to Kid Duffy of Arizona. Kid had been forced to leave Arizona owing to an unforeseen affair that had ended in a mutual drawing of guns. Two men fell badly wounded in that fracas, and only Kid rode away. Naturally the whole blame was put upon his shoulders, and the officers of the law hounded him hotly over the border and even beyond.

So Kid had kept on coming, and, when his first horse grew leg weary, he cornered and roped another in an open field, changed saddles, and went on again. When a man of any self-respect is forced to steal a horse in the West, he feels that he has done a thing infinitely worse than murder, no matter how gently the law may deal with the crime. It is hard to say how the unspoken law has grown up that deals with that offense. Perhaps it owes its origin to the fact that a man's horse often stands between him and death. He who starts to cross a burning desert toward the rich blue piles of mountains on the farther side is not at all sure how long the trip will take, and, if his horse is purloined by a treacherous comrade, he dies horribly of thirst and famine in the sands. There are many instances of just such things told commonly about the range. So there has grown up a feeling that it is as bad and definitely more dishonorable to rob a man of his horse than of his life. Therefore, murderers are left to the slow process of the law, but horse thieves are often promptly mobbed and hanged offhand.

Bearing all of this in mind, it may be understood why the temper of Kid Duffy had a razor edge when he rode into

Wooster on this evening. His position may be the better appreciated if it is understood that he had himself once officiated as hangman-in-chief at the lynching of a horse thief, and, although that fellow was a Mexican, nevertheless his body, black against the morning sky, seemed to dangle once more before the eyes of Kid.

The first thing he did was to hunt out an amiable-looking cowpuncher and inquire if there was such a thing as a drink in the town. He was taken to a place—for, after all, it was not so far from the Río Grande—where there was plenty of tequila, colorless as water and burning with a terrific and secret flame. Ten minutes later Kid Duffy walked out onto the street with the fire raging in his brain and a wicked smile of contemplation on his lips. He wanted trouble. He was hungry for it. And then it was, as he leaned against a hitching rack, that he saw young Mell walk past with that remarkable quick, soft stride.

"Who's that?" asked Kid, jerking his head over his shoulder to follow the retreating figure.

"That's Snoozer Mell. He's hell on wheels, too. If somebody was to plant him, they'd be savin' trouble for the law. You can lay to that."

Kid filed that information in the back of his hot brain. Five minutes later, when Snoozer passed again, Kid stepped out and greeted him.

"You're Snoozer Mell, I guess?" he said.

"I'm him," Snoozer replied quickly.

"Come along with me."

He expected a quick resistance, and he was amazed when the young fellow followed calmly at his side. He had no idea where to lead him except to the tequila parlor. There in the shed he invited Snoozer to drink, and Snoozer drank the first alcoholic stuff that had ever crossed his tongue and wriggled its hot way down his throat. Afterward, he coughed and choked, for tequila has the edge of a knife at the best, and this was raw stuff. That was enough for Kid.

"Maybe you don't like it," he said as he downed his own drink.

"Not much," admitted Snoozer.

"Maybe it ain't good enough for you?" continued Kid, his voice wickedly small.

Snoozer was silent.

"Maybe they's something wrong with me, too?" Kid suggested with infinite politeness.

The man behind the improvised bar slid toward the door and remained there with foxy little eyes fastened upon the pair, ready to dive backward the moment the fun began.

Again Snoozer had not a word to say, but continued to regard the other quietly with his blue eyes and his head cocked a little upon one side.

"You heard what I said?" Kid barked suddenly, his madness overwhelming him in a wave.

"I heard," said Snoozer Mell.

"Why the devil don't you answer me?"

The bartender licked his lips. It might be that the boy would take water. He really thought he would, the silence lasted so long.

"Because," said Snoozer at last, "it don't seem to me like you need an answer."

Kid grinned like a wolf when it sights a calf, staggering with weakness through the winter snow. With a whip-like left hand he struck Snoozer in the face and knocked him to a distance. With his right hand he grabbed out his gun and fired— at the thinnest of thin air. For Snoozer had flattened himself upon the floor, and, as he lay, his hand clasped an empty bottle that had once held ginger ale. He flipped it at Kid and saw it sink half its length into the stomach of that worthy. Kid

138

doubled up with a gasp and fired his second bullet squarely into the door. Then Snoozer went through the air from all fours as a cat leaps. Kid was sent crashing against the farther wall.

The bartender was long since fleeing through the outer night.

For ten fierce seconds they struggled for that gun, and, just as the sheriff came through the door, he saw Snoozer swing that same gun high in the air and crash it down upon the floor in a heap.

By the time Snoozer looked up, he was confronted by two long weapons held in the capable hands of the sheriff, with the sheriff's fighting face behind them. It was not for nothing that he had been made the controlling officer of the law in this small town. For he was as tough as he was small.

"Stick up your mitts, Snoozer," the sheriff ordered. "Stick 'em up right *pronto* and keep 'em right over your head." He licked his lips. It was surprisingly pleasant to the sheriff to have another grip with his old enemy, the boy. "This'll be about three years in the pen," he said soothingly, as he approached. "Assault with intent to kill . . . and drinkin' moonshine booze in a boot-leggin' joint!" He chuckled at the thought. "That'll be about all. About three years in the pen for you, kid. Gimme that gun!"

He reached high for it, but, in so doing, he came close to Snoozer. It should be said, in praise of the sheriff's caution, that he had rammed one of his guns into the ribs of Snoozer as he came close, but he could not be prepared for the desperation with which the boy acted. For Snoozer twitched himself to one side, knocking the gun away with the turn of his body so that it exploded into the thinnest space. The next instant his raised knee struck the sheriff's fat stomach, and, as the latter doubled over, a lifting uppercut landed beneath his chin and wafted him off his feet into a soft mist of darkness.

When the sheriff opened his eyes, his first act was to clutch at his jaw, which he thought must be broken. Then he laid his other hand on the back of his head, where he had landed on the hard flooring. Afterward, his brain cleared, and he staggered to his feet yelling the first word that came into his brain, and that first word happened to be—"Murder!"

It brought twenty men in twenty seconds.

"It's Snoozer Mell!" yelled the sheriff. "He's killed a man and assaulted me."

They ran at once to the Mell house, but no Snoozer was there. They rushed up to Snoozer's room, with Mr. Mell laboring in their wake and striving to explain that Snoozer had returned only a few moments before and had immediately departed again, carrying his blankets and his rifle along with him.

Then, from the empty room, they tore down the stairs, filling the house with the thunder of their heavy feet, and hurried out to the barn. All that they expected was there revealed as a certainty. Of the two horses that the blacksmith owned, the fastest and the toughest had been saddled with Snoozer's own saddle, and of the boy there was no trace.

They returned to the center of town to find that Kid was not killed, but still unconscious. And, five minutes later, a certain gentleman representing the long arm of Arizona's law rode into town very eager to find this same Kid Duffy.

IV

"STEVE IS A POOR LOSER"

For seven long years Wooster did not hear again of Snoozer. He had disappeared from the ken of his hometown. How many shifts of scenery he had seen in the interim it would be impossible to relate. They would need a book for their telling. Suffice it that at the end of the seventh year Snoozer Mell sat behind a table in the cool, shadowy back room of a Montana hotel and watched four ambitious gentlemen take large drafts of bootleg whisky, while he took much larger drafts of their ready cash. For the cards had proved kind to Snoozer Mell. And, to say the truth, when the cards were not kind, he found means of leading fortune gently but firmly in his direction. There are certain things that can be accomplished with a pack of cards when one practices at least two hours a day, without missing a day, and when one cultivates suppleness of fingers.

The fingers of Snoozer were, in short, very supple. His hands were so white that he had to stain them brown, together with his face. That was to make the body fit into the costume, for the costume was that of a cowpuncher, newly ridden in off the range. The ways of Snoozer, however, were his own and no other's. Nature had made him what he was, and he could not change. He was as silent as ever, and, as he sat at the table, he looked down at his cards with the same unwinking eyes, while his head was canted to one side at the same angle. Such was the attitude of Snoozer as he played and won or played and lost, and not a shadow of change occurred in his expression to tell one what went on inside his mind. He was winning steadily on this day, however, and one might have attributed his calm expression to the steadiness with which fortune favored him. Three of the four who faced him bore their losses with oaths and an occasional blow of the fist upon the table. The fourth grew pale and paler. While his three companions drank and drank to excess, he himself took only an occasional nip, as though he would bolster himself up with a false courage, and, when the small taste of whisky had stimulated him, he found the will to bet rather more largely than the others.

141

But still he lost, for he had reached the state to which he felt that, sooner or later, the luck had to turn in his favor. When a gambler reaches that point of mental opinion, he is sure to lose, for fortune cannot be either wooed or forced. She remains aloof, and it is only the aloof of mind that can win her. He grew paler, therefore, this unlucky fellow, until finally the last of his money was gone and he had placed upon the table a broad-faced, thin, gold watch, obviously an heirloom.

Snoozer allowed the other three to look it over.

"That's worth twenty dollars to this game," said one.

"Forty," said another. "Give the kid a chance to come back in. He's lost enough."

"So have I," said the third, "but we'll give him a break. Fifty dollars for the watch, eh?"

Snoozer picked it up, opened the back, and regarded it with an expert eye. "A hundred dollars," he said calmly, and pushed that sum of money across the table.

It followed the rest, and followed with dizzy speed, for the hundred dollars had looked to the loser like a capital fortune that could not be soon exhausted. In half an hour the game was ended and—"Hard luck, Steve!"—was the brief consolation that he received.

Afterward, in the narrow, barren hall of the hotel that served it as a lobby, he saw Snoozer go out.

"Who is that man?" he asked of the fellow who lounged in the nearest chair.

"Him? Don't you know him?"

"Nope. Never seen him before today."

"That's Bill Graham. Some folks say that he's got another name."

"I got an idea that he does," said Steve grimly.

"How you happen to ask about him?"

142

"Nothin'. He looks sort of different, that's all."

"Well, son, he's different, right enough. That kid has a brain on his shoulders."

"Maybe."

"No maybe about it. He's a wise youngster. Take a pack of cards, and he can make 'em talk."

"He's a youngster, eh?" Steve said, a shadow appearing between his brows.

"That's him. He's a gambler, and a damn' good one."

"Good?"

"No better. Great thing about Graham is that he plays square."

Steve grunted.

"I mean it. I've talked to a lot that have played with him. When gents play square ag'in' him, he plays square, too. But where he makes his money is when he bumps into a crook, because then he's a pile crookeder than the smartest of 'em. He can break a pack and stack it so that Noah's grandma wouldn't know that nothin' was the matter. He can stack a pack and stick a couple of crimps in it. It don't make no difference what crimp you bang into. You might miss the first of 'em. You hit the second, and it's all the same to him. He knows how the cards lie underneath it. That's the beauty of Graham! They've sent some hard ones out here to get him. But he ain't been got yet."

"Made money, eh?"

"He's got a bank account that would choke a whole herd. That's where he gets the boys that play fast and square ag'in' him. When they win, he can afford to lie low and wait. When they lose, they get busted and can't keep on. When he loses in a long session, he don't have so very much. When he wins, he might clean up a lot."

"He's got an edge either way, then."

"He's damn' decent about it, though. I've seen him stake a lot of the boys that run busted. He ain't lookin' for the small money. He's after the big stuff, and, when a crook comes along with a bankroll loaded, the kid steps out and sinks a hook into him so far that you can hear him yell a mile."

He laughed at the thought and looked up to find that Steve had not so much as smiled.

"He hangs out in this here hotel?" asked Steve.

"Sure. He's had the front room on the second floor for about a year. Everybody knows him. If he'd talk a bit more, everybody'd like him, too."

With this, as though contented and desiring to learn no more, Steve rose and stretched himself.

"All I got to say is this," he declared. "If a gent is crooked once, he's crooked all the time."

"I tell you, you're wrong about young Graham. I've told you the low-down on him."

But Steve merely grunted and left the hotel.

He did not leave it for good, however. Later in the evening he returned and marked the front of the building and how the shed that extended over the watering trough beyond made, with its sloping roof, a perfect approach and an easy one to the second floor of the building. When he had noted these things, together with the light that burned in the big window to the left, Steve departed to another quarter of the town and looked to his revolver. And when that revolver was found to be in the most perfect working condition, he dropped it back into the holster, drew his belt a notch or so tighter, took a deep breath, and returned to the front of the hotel.

All was dark in the town. The last loiterers had left the hotel itself. Up and down the street only the blank, black faces of the windows gave back the light of the stars with a few backlights. No one stirred, no voices murmured in the distance, for the entire village was soundly asleep. Even the big left window in the second story of the hotel was blank and dark.

Having made sure of this, Steve drew off his boots, tied them together, and advanced across the street. He stepped up onto the watering trough and so easily gained the roof of the shed. Up this he crawled until he was at that same left-hand window, and through this he advanced his head. Within, he felt the increased heat of the room, which the steady draft through the open window had not yet cooled. He could still smell, too, the last whiff of the cigarette that had recently been smoked, and, deciding that Bill Graham had only recently gone to sleep, Steve lay down on the roof of the shed and watched the stars. They could not tell him that what he contemplated was wrong. *Once a crook, always a crook,* he thought to himself, and comforted himself with that maxim.

As he recalled the course of the game of that evening and the steady course that it took in favor of Bill Graham, he had not the slightest doubt but that the latter had helped fortune to help him. If he took back, at the point of a revolver, some of that which Bill Graham, as the gambler was called, had taken from him, who could really blame him?

Besides, he needed that money for a purpose greater than himself. And, when he thought of that purpose, Steve became iron itself. He waited resolutely, calmly on the roof of the shed for a full half hour. Then he rose gradually to his knees, lest his moving weight should make a cracking and a creaking among the shingles. He approached the window again.

Looking in for the second time, he discovered that the air within the chamber was much cooler and the sharp sting of fresh cigarette smoke had been replaced by the heavy, sour smell of cigarette butts. Having reassured himself through a long wait that all was well for him within the room, he began to enter the window.

It was not a thing that could be accomplished in a single moment. It had to be gone about most leisurely, most carefully. He had to first press up the window a little to give himself more room. Then he had to insert one leg with the greatest care, find the floor, bring his weight to bear upon it gradually, so that there might be no creaking, and finally draw the other leg through behind him.

When all of that had been accomplished, he crouched close to the floor, where the darkness was the thickest, and surveyed the room. There, in the bed, he saw a reassuring lump under the clothes. He could not help grinning when he thought of what would go on in the mind of Bill Graham when he wakened and found the chill muzzle of a revolver jammed up beneath his chin.

He had not proceeded three careful strides toward the bed, however, when he heard a most delicate sighing sound behind him, as of a door being opened. He twitched his head around quickly, but he was too late. He only had a glimpse from the corner of his eye of the body of a man flying through the gloom of the chamber toward him. Then he was struck to the floor and gripped with iron hands.

V

"WORTH A THOUSAND"

All that a large body and well-disciplined muscles and a furious and desperate will to win could do for Steve were accomplished there in the darkness and the silence, as he struggled against his assailant. Even as he struggled, he wondered why it was that the gambler did not call for help. Was it that he feared discovery? But discovery of what? The hotel and the town seemed to be full of his friends who were willing to back him in any predicament. Certainly he would not call in vain. Yet, there was not so much as a whisper from Bill Graham.

As a matter of fact, he needed no assistance. He began to fumble for wrestling holds, and in a trice, despite all of his efforts, Steve was helpless. He could hear the soft murmur of the other through the thick blackness above him.

"You rat! You damned rat! I ought to peel off your hide in chunks! Sneak in on me in the night. . . ." As he spoke, he rose and lighted the lamp at the side of the room.

It was the most wretched hour in the life of Steve. Far sooner would he have been lying among the shadows with a bullet through his heart than to have another man look him in the face and recognize him as a thief, a sneak thief in the night. It was too horrible to keep in his mind.

In the meantime, the gambler seemed to be full of astonishment.

"You!" he exclaimed. "I thought that Jarvis . . . but it must be Jarvis, after all. Look here, kid, did Jarvis send you to get me?"

It was odd enough, this speaking down to Steve who was really two or three years his senior, but the mind of Snoozer Mell had developed beyond his years, and he thought and spoke, often, like an old man.

"Nobody sent me," declared Steve sullenly.

"Not Jarvis, that gunman, who holds a mad, unjustifiable grudge against me? Look here, Steve, I dunno much about you, but you look sort of decent to me. How much did that skunk promise to pay you for crookin' me?"

"Him! I tell you, nobody got me to come here tonight." His anger finally seemed to convince the gambler who now stepped back, nodding.

"We'll have a little talk before I turn you over to the

147

sheriff," he said. "I never had no use for sheriffs. Damn me, if they don't make me mad, just to think about 'em. So we ain't going to turn you over to 'em until we've had a chance to get at your yarn."

"There ain't no yarn," Steve stated sadly. "I . . . I just started out to do a dirty trick. I didn't see how dirty a trick it was. That's all."

During this bit of violent self-denunciation, Snoozer Mell regarded the face of his captive with the keenest interest. There could hardly have been a more boyishly open countenance. There could not have been straighter-looking eyes, steady, now filled with the anguish of self-disdain. Considering all of these details, Snoozer now liberated the heavy Colt that was on the person of the night wanderer.

"Tell me straight out, Steve," said Snoozer, "what brung you up here tonight?"

"Nothin'," said the other.

"Nothin'? Then nothin' is goin' to plant you in jail right *pronto,* and the way the judges treat burglars in these parts ain't a pretty thing, you can lay to that."

Steve sighed.

"I ain't tryin' to get nothin' on you to use in court," Snoozer said, suddenly disgusted by that thought. "All I want you to do is to give yourself a fair fightin' chance with me. I'm askin' you why you come after me tonight, if that dog Jarvis didn't sic you onto me?"

"I was busted," said Steve. He could say no more, and he watched the angry flush run over the face of Snoozer.

"Ain't you man enough to take a lickin'?" asked the gambler.

"Sure . . . if I'm beat fair and square," said Steve.

"Well?" Snoozer persisted sharply.

A less courageous man would not have dared to continue,

but Steve was without fear, and he was genuinely mastering his shame. "I heard that you was a professional," he said.

"What of it? Ain't there some honest professional gamblers that play straight with *honest* men?"

One could see that he was trembling in the very passion of his anger, but still Steve looked him fairly in the eye as he answered: "I never heard tell of any. All that I've ever seen was always crooked. That's the straight of it, so far as I know."

He thought, at first, that Bill Graham would tear the gun from the holster at his side and shoot him down, but Snoozer confronted his fury and managed to say calmly enough: "You come to get back what I'd cheated you out of."

"What I thought that you'd cheated me out of."

He watched the gambler fighting with himself during a long pause. The wind, which had been hanging in the south and east all day, had gradually swung about to the due east where it was settling with increasing force every moment. Now it picked up a swirl of dust from the street and blew it through the window. They could not see it in the blackness and by the dim lamplight, but the acrid smell of the dirt came into their nostrils.

But seven years had certainly taught Snoozer how to control himself. The swollen veins of his temples disappeared again. He was able to say in his usual quiet way: "D'you think I was markin' the cards or stackin' 'em, Steve?"

Steve shrugged his shoulders. "I ain't any expert," he said. "I don't know how things are done."

"So you come back to get what you lost?"

"Yep."

"You wanted to stick me up?"

Steve flushed and could not answer.

"About how much?"

"About five hundred."

"That's a lot. But look here, old son, that ain't the most money in the world."

"It meant a lot to me."

There was a change in Snoozer. "Maybe you got a wife back home and you meant some of that coin for her?"

"I got no wife," Steve admitted, flushing again. "Not yet."

"Hmm," murmured Snoozer. "Not yet. I ain't aimin' to pry into no private affairs, but I'm mighty interested, Steve. Tell me the straight of it."

There was something so remarkably gentle about his voice and his manner that it unlocked a secret door in the heart of Steve, and he was talking before he knew it.

"I come up north aiming to make a big stake," he began. "Not very big from your way of thinkin', maybe. A thousand would've looked like a mountain to me. I worked like the devil and got five hundred together. . . ."

"She said that she'd marry you when you got a thousand. Was that it?"

"Not just that. She ain't the kind that thinks about the coin."

"She's a new kind, then," said Snoozer.

"She is a new kind. Money don't make no difference to her. But I seen that I had to make some sort of money . . . so's we could have a good start together."

"She's used to havin' things, I guess?"

"Sort of. A millionaire wouldn't be none too good for her. How she ever come to look at me twice, I dunno. I can't make it out."

There was no sham about his humility.

"Maybe so," Snoozer said.

"But I growed up with her," Steve continued. "When she moved to a new town, I moved, too. And bein' where everybody else was a stranger to her, she took sort of kindly to me in the new town. I used to see a lot of her. Finally, when I asked her to marry me, she allowed that maybe she would. So I came north to make a stake. I got that five hundred together. But it seemed like it had took me forever. When the game started yesterday, I thought that maybe I could have a little luck and make the other half that I wanted."

"I know," said Snoozer.

"But I went bust. I was a plain fool, that's all. And on top of bein' a fool, I've played the skunk by comin' here to hold you up. I would've swore that there wasn't no such thing as a straight gambler. But I can see now. You *are* square, Graham. What would she think if she knowed what I'd done today?" He touched his pocket instinctively as he spoke.

"Lemme see her picture, if you got it there."

Steve hesitated for a moment. "It ain't something that I show around," he said at the last. "But . . . if you want to see it, Graham. . . ." He drew out a wallet. From the contents he selected a thin package of oiled silk that he unrolled and then extended the photograph to Snoozer.

Snoozer, receiving it, drew back under the yellow light of the lamp. There he studied the picture with profound care, not as something reproduced in black and white upon a piece of parchment, for there was life in the smiling face that looked out to him, and it moved Snoozer like the sound of a voice.

Snoozer looked suddenly down to the corner of the card, and then all the blood rushed from his brain back upon his heart and left him strangely pale and shaken, for there was the name of the photographer—Joe Riley—Wooster. How well he remembered little Joe Riley and his office on the second floor above Chalmers's tobacco store. He himself had sat there for his picture, bolt erect in the chair, his fists clenched to give him courage, terribly conscious of the crow's nest of hair that stared upward on the top of his head. But even the

151

strange methods of Joe Riley could not destroy the grace and the charm of this girl. She had blonde hair. That much was plain. Her smile was twisted a little to one side so that it gave her a wonderfully wistful look.

He passed the picture back to Steve, wishing with all his might that he had never seen it, for the sight of it settled a steady, small ache in his heart that he felt would never leave him until he saw the original of the photograph.

He looked again at Steve with new eyes. Whereas Steve had seemed to him before a perfectly amiable and good-natured and undistinguished youth, he seemed now like one of those predestined creatures upon whose heads the sunshine of the gods is poured forever. And, oh, that one mortal man could have received so much joy as this.

"This here girl . . . what's her name, Steve?"

"Susan. They call her Sue."

"Of course," said Snoozer.

"Susan Crane is her whole name."

"She's in Wooster now?"

"Yep."

"Suppose that you had a thousand dollars, Steve. D'you think that you could marry her dead easy?"

"She ain't the kind to break a promise. I reckon that she'd marry me without no money in my pocket at all."

Snoozer Mell stepped to the bed, where a human-shaped hump had been created by an arrangement of pillows under the blankets. From beneath the mattress he drew out a thick, well-rubbed wallet. And from the wallet he drew out a sheaf of bills. He counted out the right amount and thrust the remainder back carelessly into his pocket. It seemed to Steve the act of a millionaire; no lesser person could have handled so much hard cash with such magnificent disdain.

"Steve," Snoozer said, "I make a bargain with you. I give

you a thousand, and I turn you loose. You understand."

But Steve could only gape at him.

"What I mean," said Snoozer, "is that the sight of this picture is worth a thousand dollars to me. It ain't charity I'm givin' you."

"You mean I'm to give up Sue and . . . I'll see you in hell first!"

"I ain't a fool, Steve. Take the thousand and go back to Wooster to get her. But I'll be there before you. Is that fair and square?"

VI

"JARVIS SENDS A CHALLENGE"

It was early the next morning, while the cook was still noisily rattling at the kitchen stove and bringing down upon his head the heart-felt curses of the sleepers in the building, that Snoozer Mell, alias Bill Graham, alias many another name that had blossomed and grown too notorious in more than one section of the mountain desert, stepped out of the door onto the verandah, with his suitcase in his hand. As he issued through that doorway, an unshaven, rat-faced fellow stepped up to him.

"You're Graham?"

"I'm him."

"Here's a present for you."

He passed to Snoozer a soiled envelope, hurried to his horse at the hitching rack, and galloped away before Snoozer had more than mastered the first lines of the contents of the letter. He read:

Bill Graham:

I hear talk about you looking for me. You know that's a damn lie. I'm looking for you. And when we

meet up, we're going to have our little bust right
pronto. I've sent out three of the boys to find you. If
one of them is lucky, I'm coming right along on your
trail. You can lay to that! When I find you, Graham,
I'm going to shoot you plumb in two or else I'm
going to make you take water so's a whole town will
know that you're a yeller skunk!

Jarvis

This pleasant epistle the recipient read through twice,
carefully, looking up after the first time to note that the
messenger who had brought the note was now only a small
dust cloud on the road leading out of the town. He considered the matter carefully. With all his soul he wanted to stay
to meet Jarvis. Sooner or later, in fact, that meeting was sure
to take place.

But if he waited for Jarvis, precious days might be wasted,
and he had not a moment to lose. He had promised Steve that
he would beat him to Wooster, and, if he failed to beat Steve,
who was now warned that he stood in danger and exactly
what that danger was, Steve would promptly snap up the girl
and marry her out of hand. No, he dared not risk the delay to
await the coming of the terrible Jarvis. This retreat of his
would make much talk, and all the talk would be unfavorable
to him. Once before he had avoided Jarvis. If he avoided the
gunfighter again, it would be considered as sure cowardice. All
of this was not only very true, but it was cruelly important to
Snoozer Mell—and yet he walked on across the verandah and
to the buckboard that awaited him. For the smile of the girl,
as he remembered it, was more important than honor itself.

So the buckboard rattled him across country. Steve, he believed, would wait to catch the eastbound train that afternoon, and then, the next morning, he would start south. By

driving fourteen miles across country, Snoozer could flag a southbound express long before noon, and so gain a precious handicap in time. And what might not a few hours' start mean to him?

The buckboard brought him in two hours to his destination. An hour later, he was shooting smoothly and swiftly south with the train rocking with its speed. He carried with him all his necessities in life, boiled down to small compass like those that appear in the knapsack of a veteran soldier—or tramp. In the suitcase were his clothes for rough riding and mountain trips, his sewing kit, a book or two, and above all several packs of cards and two or three dice boxes and many dice. The consciousness that they were with him gave him a great and quiet sense of power. They were his open sesame with which he unlocked the doors that led into pocketbooks. He found himself looking up and down the quadruple row of heads that swayed and nodded before him, and the quadruple rows of faces that swayed and nodded still more stupidly behind him. They were all in his power at the time when they least looked for danger—at the very time when they began to play! He had often considered that as an ironical tribute to the powers of the gambler. And he could not look upon any crowd without feeling, keenly, that he was the master of them all.

When he reached Wooster the next day, all his sense of triumph and of power diminished to a ghost that had no reality. The sight of the familiar old street and the houses from which the sun had boiled and peeled the paint made his heart stir, but made it grow small, also. At least, the small sins of his youth would have been forgotten, by this time. Perhaps he himself would not be remembered.

He stepped in the tobacco shop to see. There was Fatty

Daniels serving behind the counter—Fatty whose face he had so battered on the day when he first went to school in Wooster.

"Hello," said the visitor.

"Snoozer!" gasped out Fatty, and leaned across the counter to shake hands.

"How's everything in Wooster?"

"Fine. Dog-gone me, if your dad wasn't in here not more'n an hour ago to get some of that plug tobacco he smokes in his pipe. I asked him if there was any word about you. He said it was seven years since he heard a whisper from you, Snoozer."

I guess that I ain't changed so much, after all, Snoozer thought to himself as he went on down the street. *Fatty recognized me mighty quick. After all, seven years ain't so much.*

Indeed, in passing down the not over-long main street of the town, he was recognized a full dozen times. Some people stopped him to shake hands. Some gasped and went hastily by him. It was very plain that his memory was green in Wooster—almost too well preserved, one might have said.

So he turned down the side street leading to his father's house. He walked two blocks, did not find it, and then turned around with a groan. He had walked straight past it without recognition, so greatly was it transformed. Once it had been a naked, graceless thing, but now it wore a new face. A little porch had been extended across the front of the building, and over the columns of this addition great masses of honeysuckle climbed to the roof and over the roof of that porch to the second story windows. It even cast some far-advanced tendrils and creepers toward the roof tree itself.

This was not the only change. Where there had once stood, between the gate and the front door, a stretch of hard-packed gravel dotted with a few shrubs, there was now a pleasant little garden. It had been newly watered, and from the soil there still sounded the faint crinkling noises that told that the roots were yet drinking. It was Saturday evening, but, even so, Harrison Mell was not in the habit of leaving the blacksmith shop until sundown on any day. Therefore, he surely had not left his place of work to tend the garden at this early hour. There was only one explanation. Harrison Mell was married!

Of course that garden was a woman's conception. Who else could have thought of it and then given the time to the tending of it? He had married, and, if his new wife had planted yonder sprawling honeysuckle vine, surely the marriage must have taken place as soon as Snoozer left.

He waited till he got me out of the way, Snoozer thought bitterly to himself, *and then he married again. He forgot my mother.*

At that very moment the tall form of his father came around the corner of the house. His hat was off, and the rays of the setting sun cast a rosy light through the tousled mop of hair. It had been iron gray when Snoozer last saw it. It was the purest white now. Yet there was no stoop to the shoulders of Harrison Mell. In spite of his white hair he seemed even taller and broader than ever before; he was like a Hercules from whom time cannot take the strength. Strangest of all, in his hand he carried a hoe, and his sleeves were rolled up to the huge elbows. Harrison Mell had turned gardener, indeed.

He's married to a younger woman, Snoozer thought instantly. *And she makes him take care of the garden. That's it.*

"Dad!" he called ahead.

Harrison Mell neither answered nor moved to greet the returned prodigal. He merely leaned upon the hoe and dropped one hand upon his hip. Then, as Snoozer came through the gate: "Dog-gone me if it ain't Snoozer come back ag'in!"

They shook hands, eyeing one another.

"Hold on, Dad. My hand ain't iron."

"Sorry, if I hurt you, boy," said Harrison Mell.

"You're lookin' fine, Dad."

"I ain't feelin' so bad. You're lookin' prosperous."

"I've made some money."

"How?"

There was only an instant of hesitation, then Snoozer twitched back his shoulders, for he had never been one to put his best foot forward. Let the world take him as it pleased, he would not lie about himself.

"Gambling," he said tersely. He felt the glance of his father wander swiftly over his face.

"Come in an' rest yourself. You got your things in that bag?"

"But who done all this, Dad?"

"Me."

"I mean the planting, and all that?"

"Me. Come on in, Snoozer."

They passed beneath the honeysuckle through a curtain of heavy fragrance. They sat down in the living room. This, at least, had not changed, and the first lightning glance of Snoozer went to a certain place on the wall. Yes, there hung the picture of his mother as before.

"I didn't know you liked gardens," Snoozer said more amiably, for, since he had seen that picture, he had decided that the new wife was at least a tolerant woman.

"I didn't, either," said the father. "But after you left, it sort of give me something to do."

What a world of confession was contained in that brief sentence—of loneliness, of a restless turning of the spirit here and there, until at last those iron hands found occupations in the making of a garden. Snoozer Mell turned the thought

158

slowly in his mind. But, still, he could not understand. He had thought that he knew his father as one knows the face of a rock. Now he found himself grasping toward new conceptions, and they were all beyond his touch.

VII

"SNOOZER MEETS SUSAN"

He had barely time to deposit his suitcase in his room, when he heard a girl's voice calling from the street: "Uncle Harrison! Oh, Uncle Harrison!" It was a most amazing thing that any woman should call upon that burly father of his, unless it were to call him forth to shoe a horse. But that he should be addressed as Uncle Harrison was as marvelous as the garden that bloomed in the front yard and the honeysuckle vine that swarmed with its blossoms across the front of the old building. Here was a new man, apparently, to whom he had come home—a maker of gardens, a patron of young girls with lovely voices.

He went downstairs, and, looking through the darkness of the hallway, he saw her in front of the house in the rose of the sunset, framed by the gently swinging trailers of the honeysuckle vine. There came a knock at the heart and the soul of Snoozer Mell, as when an unbeliever sees heaven revealed. For this voice that had called him down came from the very woman whose picture had drawn him back to the town. But, oh, how different from any picture she was! There was the same faintly whimsical and twisted smile, and the same lift of the head that he had seen in the photograph, as though she were brimming over with a secret inward happiness. These things were the same, and he could recognize them in her. But he felt that after this, no matter where he came near her, he would know her presence by the leap of his heart.

Let another call the glimpse of her coincidence, since the

town was small and all the inhabitants were known to one another. Let another call it coincidence, but to Snoozer, it was downright fate, and by that chance coming she was set apart in a sort of holy light from all that he had seen or known in his life.

His father came out to her from behind the house, calling: "Sue! Where you been, girl? Ain't you been forgettin' me?"

She took his arm and laughed up into his face. And Snoozer caught his breath. He had never seen another human being dare to use his father so familiarly. But she, so close to the big man, and with her kindness fairly breathing forth upon him, seemed to know him better than all others had ever known him. Even Snoozer's mother had not known her husband so well, and Snoozer could remember how she used to sit over her sewing in the evening and lift timid eyes, now and again, toward the big man fenced away from the rest of the family by his raised newspaper. For he was one of those silent men who love political news and who, reading the stilted and florid phrases of some stump speaker rehearsed in the paper, feel the springs of muted eloquence loosed and swelling in the throat. Snoozer had never guessed it; neither had Snoozer's mother. They had formed a league for mutual understanding, a sort of secret alliance of tenderness to make up for what they missed in the master of the house.

"I've been very busy sewing, and making a dress," she was saying.

"*Humph!*" said Harrison Mell. "The Wooster boys is what's been makin' you busy, Sue. Don't tell me!"

"Not one of them. I ain't seen a one," said Sue.

"You wouldn't cross your heart on that?"

"Oh, but wouldn't I, though?"

"You ain't seen a one of 'em?"

"Not a one."

"The louts!" said Harrison Mell. "I dunno what's the matter with the young gents of this day. They ain't like they used to be. Maybe they figger that Steve owns you, Sue, and they ain't wastin' no time. Ain't you been asked to the dance tonight?"

"No."

"Well . . . darn!"

"But I don't care a bit."

The blacksmith groaned again. "If I was a young spark," he said, "I'd show 'em."

"Would you come courtin', Uncle Harrison?"

"Wouldn't I, just? I'd be settin' in your parlor every evenin', wishin' that I could find something to say."

And they laughed together in what seemed to Snoozer a delightful harmony, the thin, sweet soprano over the rumbling bass.

"The sweet peas are comin' out again," she noted.

"You picked all the pods off for me," said Harrison Mell. "That brings 'em out ag'in. I told you that it would. Why ain't you made a garden for your own house, Sue?"

"Dad hasn't much interest, you know. And I haven't, either. All my heart is over here in your garden, Uncle Harrison. Because it's so beautiful."

"Nope. They's a dozen in town that's a lot finer than mine."

"But they haven't made it the way you have. When I go by this place, I always see you in the garden, Uncle Harrison. . . ." She stopped short, for there was Snoozer coming down the front steps, with his head a little to one side and with his short, quick, silent step.

"This here is my boy . . . Snoozer . . . I mean, his name is Alfred."

Snoozer, astounded, recalled that this was the first time in his life that his father had ever found it necessary to call him by his first name. She was saying that she was very happy to see Uncle Harrison's boy. And he was murmuring something in answer. He hardly knew what. Where had he been all this time, she wished to know?

"Him? He's been wanderin'," said the blacksmith hastily. "Been wanderin' all around. Snoozer likes to see things."

She nodded at Snoozer kindly. It was plain to see that she was making ready to open the doors of her mind freely to him, as the son of Uncle Harrison. Harrison Mell went away to put up the horses, and the boy and the girl talked for a time.

"Did Dad make this here garden after you come to town?" asked Snoozer Mell.

"Oh, no! It was almost the way it is now, when I first came. The honeysuckle . . . well, it was up to the eaves, I guess."

She put a finger upon her lips, in thoughtful recollecting, and Snoozer found himself breathing hard. For how delicately and purely she was made, as though the creator had lavished upon her enough dainty care to have furnished forth a dozen other girls with charms.

"I thought an idea like this might have come from you," he explained.

She looked up at him, half smiling, a little aloof, seeing the compliment.

"I'll have to be goin'," she said, grown rather shy.

"I'll see you home," Snoozer said calmly, and went through the gate beside her.

They walked in silence through three blocks, and every step of the way the silence grew thicker, but still he could find not a word to say until they came to the gate of her cottage. He told himself that he had been a fool, and, as he said good bye, his face was red. She was a little flushed, also, no doubt in anger at his silence.

"I hear that there's some talk about a dance tonight," said Snoozer.

"Yes, there is."

"Are you goin'?"

"I dunno," Sue answered, looking aside.

Was she hiding a smile of decision from him?

"Will you come with me?" Snoozer asked hoarsely.

"Oh," cried the girl, "do you want me to? Really?"

He grew still redder. "I do," said Snoozer.

"I'd love to go. But . . . it doesn't seem right."

"Why not?" he asked sharply.

"Uncle Harrison's son . . . taking a girl to a dance." She laughed suddenly. "I'm sure Uncle Harrison never went dancing."

"I'm not Uncle Harrison, you see," said Snoozer. "What time'll I come?"

"About half-past eight. It begins at nine, I guess."

"Good bye."

"Good bye."

He went back home in a haze of doubt. In the kitchen his father was cooking supper.

"You go in an' sit down," said Snoozer. "I'll manage things. I ain't forgot how to cook."

His father lifted his brows at this authoritative voice and hesitated. Then he meekly went into the other room and sat down to his paper.

When they were at the table, there was no talk until finally Snoozer said: "You and Sue seem pretty thick, Dad."

"Her?" Harrison said, bringing his eyes back from some distant dream. "Sue? She's a angel, Snoozer."

There was another long pause. Snoozer did not break it until he was rising to clear away the dishes.

"Me and Sue are goin' to the dance tonight, together," he said.

"Hey?" cried the blacksmith, half starting from his chair.

It was to Snoozer a greater shock than a pair of revolvers leveled at his head, that surprise and disapproving horror of his father.

"Ain't I good enough to take her?" Snoozer asked bitterly.

"You!" cried the father with a wealth of meaning in his voice. "Well," he added in a milder tone, "nobody ain't good enough for her. Steve is a clean boy. But nobody ain't good enough for Sue. Well, you go along and take her!"

While Snoozer did the dishes, he heard his father tramp out of the house. *It even riles him to have me take the girl to a dance,* Snoozer said to his gloomy heart.

When he had finished with the dishes, he went up to prune himself for the dance. Nothing could ever make him good-looking, he told himself as he looked into the mirror and saw the perennially serene boyish face, with the spot of high color in either cheek. To the end of his life that amiable and half-childish face would attract bullies as honey attracts bees. To the end of his life he would have his fights. That side of it was not unattractive. But what would Sue think of him? He had never cared what other women might have in mind when they considered him. Now there was a vital difference.

When he went downstairs, his father rose from his rocking chair and left it canting back and forth, the shoulder pad flapping with its swing. He held out a little bouquet of yellow roses, all chosen buds and tightly wrapped with the virgin newness of life.

"Maybe you'd like to take these along to Sue."

"Thanks," Snoozer said, marveling again. He added: "Does Miss . . . I mean, does Sue know . . . about . . . me?"

His father sighed and answered: "I dunno. I ain't been talkin' about you."

So Snoozer departed in solemn thought. He could not have asked for a more convincing proof of his father's coldness toward him. This was the last blow—that he should not have talked to the girl of his own son.

VIII

"AT THE DANCE"

He went with an orphaned feeling that he had lost his father at the last, and, when he reached the house of the girl, she came to him like a balm for his aching hurt and, looking up into his face, perhaps she, too, saw the sorrow and the loneliness that were there. For her own face grew gentle and a little sad.

He held the bouquet stiffly forth. "Maybe you'd wear these?" he said.

She made a little outcry over them, like a delighted child. He watched her hold them forth at different angles, admiring them. He watched her place them against her rose-colored dress while she demanded of him if the stiff yellow blossoms and the green of the leaves did not go perfectly against that background. Snoozer knew nothing of color harmonies, but he agreed that they went well enough. He would have agreed to anything and everything.

"You were mighty good to bring them!" she said.

That cruel soul of honesty that belonged to Snoozer stabbed him and forced him to say coldly: "Dad picked 'em . . . he thought about having me bring 'em."

At this she looked swiftly up to him, a little hurt, trying to smile at him and finding it difficult. But a moment later she was gay again as she pinned the flowers on her dress and put on her coat. If she had only been a little slower, he could have helped her, he told himself.

A new torture came to him on the way to the ball, for, if he wished to woo her, what sheerest madness it was to take her to this public place where, the instant they appeared together, a thousand tongues would begin to buzz against him, and all the wicked past would rise up and look him in the face while the townsfolk chattered softly a thousand warnings to her. However, he had committed himself. It was too late to draw back. On the way, he fought the matter over with himself. It was best to tell her with his own lips, and yet the story would take so long, and he talked so poorly. The result was that they walked the entire distance to the hall in the bleakest silence, and the silence itself was a torment. But just before they reached the place he managed to say: "I'm sorry I ain't a better talker."

"Oh," she said, "I don't mind. That's like Uncle Harrison."

He sighed. "Inside, you'll hear a lot of bad things about me. I guess that they're mostly true."

And with that, looking grimly straight before him, he helped her through the doorway with so stern a hand that she could not answer him, although he felt her questioning, half frightened, half protesting eyes fixed on his face.

They left her wrap in the coatroom. Then they stepped into a blare of music that filled the air like a mist, it seemed to Snoozer. Yet he stepped off into the dance with her. The motion helped to clear his brain, and now he could see their faces. They were all watching. They were all either aghast or smiling covertly and whispering. It was going to be much worse than he had expected.

At least the youth of the town seemed glad enough to see Sue. They swarmed about her after the dance ended. She was engaged in a trice for the next dance and the next and the next, so Snoozer picked out the homeliest and the kindest face in the room, which was that of Jessie Brown, and, going up to her, he said: "Have you forgotten me, Jessie?"

"I guess not," Jessie answered without emotion. "I guess nobody's forgot you, Snoozer."

"Will you dance this next one?"

The head of Jessie rose a little higher. "I guess I got it taken," she said, and looked past him, or through him.

Snoozer retreated toward the doorway very slowly, with his head canted a bit upon one side and his eyes wandering from the face of one man to another, watching their covert smiles disappear in blank seriousness and thought.

He went out into the air and smoked a cigarette, tasting not the smoke but the bitterness of his soul. Then he went back inside the hall, and the first thing he saw was little Mary Kearney, looking him over boldly as she whirled past, and then laughing in his face, while her partner bit his lip to control a smile. That would be it, of course. The men dared not, but the women were privileged to stab as they pleased.

He saw Sue dancing in the midst of the crowd, her head very high, and her face very flushed. Of course, she had heard everything about him by this time, for that must be her third partner. The knees of Snoozer weakened as a cold weight formed in the pit of his stomach. He felt a vast desire to turn and bolt for the quiet shelter of his father's house. Even old Atkins on the musicians' platform, swaying and nodding and grinning to the jerky rhythm of the ragtime, seemed to be grinning at Snoozer.

Then, suddenly, Sue was before him saying good bye to her partner.

"I'm a little sick. I guess I'll have to go," he heard her say, and the slick-haired youth grinned and departed with a side glance at the ominous figure of Snoozer. Then she came to Snoozer.

"Will you take me away?" she said.

When they were outside, she would doubtless tell him her mind concerning his effrontery in taking her to a public dance in that town where everyone knew all about him. He helped her into her wrap and followed her as she ran down the steps and into the chill, black air of the night. Down the sidewalk she hurried with quick, irregular steps, like one in a passion of anger. And Snoozer still followed weakly.

When would she pause to storm at him? Not till she reached the security of her own home, it seemed. Perhaps she feared him, otherwise. Perhaps even the women in Wooster feared him now. He blinked hard and went on. They reached the gate of her house. They passed down the garden path.

Then she paused suddenly. "Oh," she cried, taking one of his hands in her cold fingers, "how could they talk like that?"

Snoozer stared humbly down at her, white of face. "I shouldn't've took you," he said huskily.

"I hate them! I hate them all!" cried Sue.

"Wait a minute," Snoozer said, dazed. "Look here. I guess they didn't tell you nothing that wasn't true."

"No, no, no!"

Snoozer took a deep breath. It seemed the first he had drawn in whole minutes, and the cold night air was thrilling nectar. Suddenly the whole world came to life joyously. All had been standing still, waiting and watching, but now the broad branch above them stirred to the wind, and the stars began to dance and shine. And here was a voice of dearest music, saying: "I don't believe one word of it, Alfred."

That imp of the perverse that had ever lived in him came to life, also, and spurred him on.

"They didn't make it black enough. They didn't know, even, that I'm a gambler, Sue. You understand? Professional gambler."

Then he waited, looking down in her face, but seeing nothing and feeling each second fall upon him with a great and greater weight.

"Oh," she said at last, "you're so honest . . . and so brave."

"No," he said eagerly. "Look here, I don't want you to think. . . ."

"Besides, you're the son of Uncle Harrison."

"He's a mighty lot better man than me."

"Oh, he's the best man in the world, of course. But I . . . I wish they were all dead! Oh, they laughed at you, Alfred, and you had to stand there and bear it and look them in the face, and all because you were trying to make me happy, and torturing yourself."

"That's not it. You see. . . ."

"Hush!"

He was silent.

"Look at me, Alfred."

He stared wonderingly down at her.

"The men didn't dare. It was only the women . . . the cowards, the cowards! If I could only make it all up to you. . . . Good night, Alfred."

He reached for her hand, dumb with happiness, but she slipped in close to him, and two swift arms were around his neck, and warm, trembling lips were touched against his own, and then she was gone with a frightened whispering of skirts into the house, and the screen door shut behind her.

Snoozer went drunkenly out of the yard and to his father's house. It was all because she pitied him, he told himself with a fierce determination to see nothing but the truth. Yet in spite of that determination, joy kept welling up in his heart from a hundred springs. He could not fight it back, and it lifted his soul and washed it away into a dizzy heaven full of music and delirious happiness. He began to count and recount the hundred parts of that last half second when she had kissed him.

Suddenly he looked up to the lofty black sky of the night with the stars hanging low and white in it, and it seemed to Snoozer that he knew, at last, that there was a God beyond those stars who used them like eyes to watch the lives of men. And he swore to himself that God above the high arch of eternity should see from that instant a different man walking in the body of Snoozer Mell. No, that name would no longer do. For she had called him what even his mother had not called him, since those infant days when he used to fall asleep so soundly at the supper table and be carried, half senseless, to his bed and the pleasant chill of the welcoming sheets. Even his mother had forgotten his name, it seemed, but Sue had recalled it and given with it new birth to him.

He went on, uncertain in his footing, breathing with hot resolves. Steve was still in his way. Well, Steve did not matter. No matter who married her, all that counted was that he should always love her. But, of course, she was as far too good for him as a saint from heaven.

Behind him followed a long, heavy stride to which he paid no attention until it turned in behind him through the gate of his father's house. Then he turned and looked back at a tall, ponderous figure.

"Is that you, Dad?" he called.

There was no answer. Instead, Harrison Mell strode up the steps, cast the door open, and with an extended, enormous arm pointed him into the house. Snoozer meekly obeyed and went in.

"FATHER AND SON QUARREL"

Snoozer was overawed. In all his life he could not remember that his father had ever before lost his temper so completely. Indeed, now that he remembered the past, he could see that he had been in constant dread of the big man because of his silent ways and his formidable appearance, not because Harrison Mell had ever been really severe.

The door closed behind him so heavily that the house shuddered. Then he turned about in the lamplight and confronted his father. There was no doubt about it, the blacksmith was in a black fury. He shook with it. His face worked with it. His long, thick fingers thrust out and contracted like spasmodic movements of a spider's legs. There was one ridiculous detail, although Snoozer did not think of that until later. This was that the spectacles of the blacksmith had quite slipped from the bridge of his nose and now hung from his ear by one guard only, in imminent danger of falling off.

"I seen everything," Harrison Mell announced.

"Yes?" Snoozer said, because he could think of nothing else to say.

"I thought I told you that Sue was engaged?"

"I guess you did tell me, Dad."

"Then, by heaven, Snoozer, I was dreamin' . . . I wasn't seein' straight when I . . . when I seen you makin' love to her?"

"Me?" Snoozer cried, full of innocence.

His father's eyes started from their sockets. "You sayin' that you didn't?"

"Me? Never a single word!"

The smile of the blacksmith was concentrated with exquisite fury. "I got no eyes, maybe?" he suggested fiercely, but quietly.

"I dunno," persisted Snoozer. "All I know is that I didn't say a word."

"You didn't have to talk, maybe?" asked the father sneeringly. "You just had to look at her, maybe, and then you could kiss her whenever you wanted to?"

Snoozer sighed. If he had been told this thing before, he would have denied it sternly and steadily. It was impossible that his father should have been a spy, and yet a spy he most certainly had become.

"It didn't mean nothin' . . . that kiss," said Snoozer.

"I got no doubt that it didn't . . . to you."

"Dad, will you just listen to me?"

"While you tell me that she ain't nothin' to you . . . and her kisses ain't nothin'. . . ."

"No, while I tell you how she. . . ."

The old man gasped for breath, and, finding it, he said: "'Don't talk no more. Don't talk no more. I got to think. Gimme a chance to think it out."

He could be seen to struggle desperately, an inward struggle, as he fought for the right thing to do. At length he could say simply: "I ain't fitted to be no judge of nobody. I'm a mighty simple man, Snoozer."

Snoozer said not a word, but waited, with his eyes upon the door, for so great was the emotion of his father that he would not have been surprised if tears had begun to trickle down from his eyes into his bristling mustaches, which were as black as his hair was white.

He could not see his father so shamed, yet that very emotion was a revelation, and he could not tell whether he most pitied or loved or reverenced this man.

"What comes first," said the blacksmith, "is that you ain't

no honest man. I guess that's plain."

Snoozer lifted his head a little.

"I guess that's plain," the blacksmith repeated. "Everybody in Wooster says that you'll come out worse than bad, and I guess that they ought to be right. You done some pretty bad things before you left here. Then you come back after seven years, when a man might think that you'd had a chance to see what was what and to settle down. But you come back a gambler."

He paused. His grief seemed to be greater than his anger now, but still Snoozer, for all the power of his will and all the courage of his heart, could not meet or bear for a single instant those blazing eyes.

"Must all gamblers be crooked?" he asked.

"You tell me," said the blacksmith. "You've seen some of 'em?"

"Of course."

"Ever find a honest one before?"

Snoozer bowed his head. After all, it was bitterly true. He had never met one whom he would not have treated as cruelly as a shark.

"Maybe you're different from all the rest?" asked his father.

Snoozer could not answer.

"But you comin' back like this, what d'you do? You pick out a girl that's an angel, Snoozer, and you start in. . . . Snoozer, what did you want to do with her?"

Snoozer jerked up his head at last, for he had been persecuted too much and was whipped now into a corner.

"What do most gents want when they find the right sort of a girl?"

"They want to act honorable!"

"I say so, too."

"Bah!" sneered the old man.

"I say it, and I mean it."

"I've heard fine talk before. You ain't the first one. Talk is mighty easy. Talk is mighty cheap. What was in the insides of your heart when you was with her? Tell me that!"

Snoozer answered hardly louder than a whisper. "Dad, I loved her."

It acted strangely upon his father, as though a drop of poisonous and burning acid had fallen upon his flesh.

"You love her?" he floundered.

"Yes."

"Look at me."

"I'm listenin', Dad."

"I tell you, I love her, too. I love her like she was my own girl, born to my own wife and raised and loved by my own hands. You hear me, Snoozer?"

How could he fail to hear the terrible thunder of that voice? It ran and bounced in his ears. It must be flooding through the air a whole block away.

"I hear you, Dad."

"I say I love her, and I say you don't. . . ."

"Dad, you got to listen."

"I got to listen? I'll see you go to the devil first! I know what you mean by her. I tell you, I'd lay you a dead man on the floor before I'd let you come near her again! You'll leave this here town. You'll never come back. You hear me, Snoozer?"

What shall one say of the things that were passing through the mind of Snoozer? For, in the first place, he felt in himself a warmer and a truer love for his father than ever before. If only he could explain in simple words that the girl had not been kissed by him—that she herself had taken the initiative—that she had kissed him out of the boundless goodness of her heart, and not because of any tender emotion more than pity.

But he could not say these things. In the first place, he could not find the adequate words with which to express himself. In the second place, even if he found the words, he could never make his father believe them. There was nothing for him to do but to stand quietly. That wicked devil, the imp of the perverse, was rising in him and taking control of him.

"I hear you, Dad," he said. "I'll tell you just this . . . I ain't goin' to leave Wooster, and you can make up your mind to that."

"What?"

"They can't run me out. When she marries this sneak Steve. . . ."

"Sneak? You ain't worthy of lickin' his boots. He's an honest boy and a good, hard-workin' boy."

"I say that he's a cur. He'll let the gent that's knocked him down pick him up ag'in. Is that a man?"

"You know nothin' about him. I don't want to hear what you think about him, neither! You hear me, Son?"

"I hear you. But why ain't I got a right to talk out what's inside of me?"

"Because what you say ain't no good. By heaven, I begin to see through the whole of you. They's no good in you . . . they's no good in you."

It was partly a wail of passion, and it was partly a cry of grief. And, oh, how the soul of Snoozer quailed and shrank within him. He felt as though he had been torn in vain by that wild, new voice of the blacksmith. Out of his own agony he answered blackly: "If you see right through me and there ain't no good in me, then there ain't no use to me trying to act no part. I'll be whatever's bad in me. Sue. . . ."

"Don't use her name!" thundered the father. "It ain't right

nor fittin' that you should be speakin' her name like that!"

"I tell you, I'll see Sue every day. . . ."

"You . . . cur!" cried the father, raising a great fist above his head.

"This gent, Steve, if he dares to show his face when I'm around this here town of Wooster . . . I'll cut him in two. If you see him, you can tell him that."

"You're going to try to get Sue?" gasped out the father, his whole huge frame swinging from side to side with his grief and his despair and his fury.

"I am!" cried Snoozer.

"For what? In heaven's name, for what?"

"For what?" Snoozer repeated, or the devil that was in him. "For what I please, that's all."

There rose from the lips of the great blacksmith a yell of torment and rage. He reached out frantically. There was a long-lashed riding quirt hanging on the wall. He plucked it away, tearing the nail with a screech from its socket. He flung the lash above his head and whipped it down across the face of Snoozer, again and again.

What followed was perhaps only a reflex action. Through the shower of stinging slashes, Snoozer struck home with all the smoothly oiled power of supple body and thickly muscled shoulders.

He saw the big man totter like a wall that goes down in the storm. Then he fell and lay sprawling, one huge arm hanging across the seat of a chair, and his head lopped over on the loose shoulder.

X
"JARVIS STILL ON SNOOZER'S TRAIL"

As one flees from the threatened ruin of a staggering house, so fled Snoozer and stood by the gate, staring back at his father's house with wild eyes. He could never cross that threshold again, he knew. Not even though all his clothes, all his money, even all those well-thumbed tools of his trade were left in his room behind him.

Then swift emotion struck at him, and he began to see things as in the rifts of lightning that crack the sky in a thunderstorm and blackness still more terrible, and show the low-flying mists, dark as smoke, the trailing fingers of the storm. So it was with Snoozer, standing there in the quiet night, and feeling hell within him, and seeing heaven above him, and all the bright hope of it lost.

He had struck down his father with his own hand. Perhaps he had killed him. He remembered the limp manner in which the blacksmith had lain, and he was about to rush back into the house and look at the fallen man again, but he had only to recall the prodigious thews and sinews of Harrison Mell. No such a giant of a man, such a Hercules, although his limbs might be unstrung by the shock of a single blow, could have been killed by it.

Snoozer wandered out of the town and through the fields. How far he walked or what he had in mind he could not have said, except that he knew he must keep in motion to escape from the horror that was in him, for he had struck his father with his own hand.

He could not have told how long he wandered, but at length some reason returned to him. He must go back to the town, buy a horse, ride away, and never again must he see Wooster or the face of the girl. For she would know. Nothing could keep her from knowing. After that, he could only pray that he would never have to confront the scorn and the anger in her eyes.

He went straight back toward old Gus Bauer's livery

stable. Gus always had a few horses to sell, and he would be sure to pick up a fairly good animal there. He avoided streets and cut across vacant lots and through back yards to get to the place.

He was wise, indeed, in having avoided the public places for, when he reached the front of the building, he learned that the news had already spread through the town. He could hear the voice of old Gus replying to young Adolph, his son, who had brought the tidings. Snoozer leaned against the wall beside the sliding door and listened.

"How come the fight?" said Gus.

"I dunno," Adolph responded.

"Maybe Snoozer was drinkin'."

"Most like. I seen him lookin' pretty green up to the dance hall. I guess that he wanted to forget the way the folks treated him up there."

"Wooster ain't got no place for gents like him, Adolph. Now he starts in beatin' his own father."

"Don't seem possible that *anybody* could have downed big Mell."

"Maybe he used a gun butt. That's about what happened. What does the doc say about Harrison Mell?"

"He dunno just what to say. It's a stroke, you see."

"A which?"

"Well, paralyzed in parts, or something like that. I dunno just what. Maybe he'll never be able to walk ag'in."

"That's the devil. What'll they do to Snoozer?"

"Some says that he had ought to be lynched. I dunno what'll happen. Lynchin' wouldn't be none too good for him."

"What does Harrison Mell want?"

"He don't want nothin' that he can say. Seems like he can't talk much."

Snoozer shrank back into the darkness and sat down with his chin resting upon his hands, very sick and very lonely of spirit, for now his punishment had truly come upon him.

He began to think it over, fumbling his way from point to point, uncertainly. He thought at first only of his flight. Then he began to see that someone must remain behind to take care of the invalid and to provide for him. When that occurred to him, he knew that his fate had come upon him, for to stay in Wooster would now, for him, be to stay in hell itself.

He rose and went straight back to the house of Harrison Mell. At the outer gate he paused and looked around him, slowly, at the trees, at the black sky, at the swirl of stars. He drew in a great breath filled with the fragrance of the garden. For it seemed to Snoozer that this was the last time he could ever enjoy the beauty of the world with a free heart. Then he went into the house.

In the hall he encountered Sue, carrying something neatly arranged on a tray, with a sprig of green stuff and a blossom or two. She stopped short and looked at him as if she expected a blow, but Snoozer went straight up the stairs to his father's room.

He heard a faint, wild cry from below: "Doctor Bostwick?"

The old doctor met him at the door, a squat, thick bulldog of a man.

"You here?" he said to Snoozer. "You here. How dare you come back and show your face? Wooster is no place for you, young man. You aren't needed, and you aren't wanted in this town. As a matter of fact," he added significantly, "this place is no longer healthy for you. The air is sure to be bad for you, Snoozer. If I were you, I'd leave at once and never come back."

"I've heard you talk," said Snoozer. "Now let me through this door."

"To finish what you've begun?" cried the doctor. "Snoozer, I'm armed, and, if you try to come through that door, you'll have to do a second murder."

"A second murder!" Snoozer cried in an indescribable voice.

"Yes. What you've done already is worse'n murder. I don't think that he'll ever walk again."

Snoozer leaned against the wall for a moment, until his heart cleared. Then he stepped close, and, taking the doctor under the armpits, for all his weight lifted him smoothly and gently to one side and stepped into the chamber. There lay Harrison Mell stretched in bed with his huge, long arms stretched upon the covers beside him and his eyes closed.

There was something in those closed eyes that struck Snoozer more terribly than the most accusing glance or the most ringing words. He would have given a year of happy life to have been able to find words and to speak them, then. But all he could do was to say: "Dad, maybe you'd like to have the paper read to you?"

He waited, trembling. He did not know it, but he had backed against Dr. Bostwick, and was clutching him for support with a violence that left black and blue spots upon that honest physician. But even the doctor did not feel the pain at the moment. He was waiting, as Snoozer was waiting. Then the eyes opened, and the lips parted, and the breast of the giant heaved.

All he said very calmly was: "I'd be tolerable glad to hear the news, Snoozer."

The doctor tiptoed from the room. He stole down the stairs before Snoozer's voice began, and in the hall beneath he found the girl, still fighting herself to get enough courage to take her up the stairs.

"You better wait for half an hour," he said.

"You haven't left him . . . not with . . . his son?" she asked the doctor.

"There's nothing to fear," said Dr. Bostwick. "Between you and me, I should not be surprised if the heaviest blow has fallen on young Snoozer."

And he went out of the house, leaving her agape behind him.

After a time she stole up the stairway to reconnoiter cautiously, and she heard the soft voice of Snoozer reading the daily news patiently, steadily. She listened, awestruck. It reminded her of an old fable of a lion that became the companion of a man, and then, feeling as though those blue, blank eyes of Snoozer were looking straight down upon her, she shrank away downstairs and waited again.

Ten minutes later a silent crowd marched upon the Mell house. There were perhaps a hundred men in the assemblage, and each was masked and each was armed. They reached the gate to the garden, and there they were met by the doctor.

"If he deserved hanging," Bostwick said, "you wouldn't be able to find him here. You'd have to ride to catch him. My friends, give the Mell boy another chance. He's upstairs now, reading the paper to his father."

Having said this, he did not remain to argue, but wisely took his way through the crowd and to his own home. The crowd waited, then a whisper and a deep-throated murmur went through it, and finally it began to dissolve at the outskirts and fade away into the night. One half-resolute knot remained, for half an hour, doubtful, but, when they saw that their numbers had shrunk to half a dozen, they thought of still another thing, and that was the old record of Snoozer as a warrior. That record was enough to hasten their steps away.

A stranger chapter was written in the morning. At eight o'clock, punctually, Harrison Mell had always joined his old partner, Loomis, in the blacksmith shop. And at eight o'clock, punctually, on this morning, Snoozer appeared.

"Dad can't come," he said to the startled Loomis. "I've come to help out, if you'll use me."

"Me?" thundered Loomis, springing up. "What in the devil do you mean by comin' to me to . . . ?" Here he fell silent, and then he added suddenly: "What d'you know about blacksmithin'?"

"Nothing," said Snoozer.

"Well," said Loomis, "take off your coat. Maybe you can learn."

Afterward, many men and women in Wooster found occasion to walk past the door of the blacksmith shop, slowly, and glancing in, they saw Loomis holding the hot iron bar in one hand and tapping with a guiding hammer with the other while the great fourteen-pound sledge swung lightly in the powerful hands of Snoozer and rained smashing blows upon the designated places.

At noon, when Snoozer walked home to cook lunch for himself and his father, he passed Sue, walking up the street with Steve. And they both went past him without a word.

But that's only a part of it, Snoozer to himself. *That's only a beginnin'.*

"I thought you'd gone," said Harrison Mell, when Snoozer carried the lunch upstairs to him.

"I was over to the shop," Snoozer explained. "I'm learning the trade from Loomis."

Upon that subject they talked no more, but Snoozer went about the room, tidying things here and there and making all neat. Then he opened the window wider and drew in some of the trailers of the honeysuckle vine and arranged them with wires along the wall.

"Maybe that's more cheerful, Dad," he said, and went back to his work at the forge.

His hands were sore, and blisters were beginning to pull out on them, but he told himself that all pain was welcome. Pain was to be his portion in body and soul from now on, and the sooner he was inured to it the better. Before the close of the day, Loomis finally said: "Well, Snoozer, you keep tryin' like that. You got a knack to you."

Snoozer looked down to his bleeding hands and answered not a word. But just as he was leaving the shop, a tall man with an unshaved, dirty face and outrageous rags for clothes stood before him.

"They's a friend of yours waitin' for you downtown that would be mighty glad if you was to come to meet him, Graham."

"Who?" asked Snoozer.

"Jarvis," said the other, and, grinning malignantly, he turned away and mounted his horse again.

XI

"FOR HIS FATHER'S SAKE"

The great tragedy to Snoozer was not the thing that came afterward, terrible as that might have seemed to another. It was in the battle that he fought out with himself as he started home. But before he had walked down the length of the first block, his mind was made up, and he knew that he must not venture to face Jarvis. He had small doubt of himself. He could kill Jarvis if he faced him; he had always felt that he could dispose of Jarvis at his will, but he had never had the instinct of a killer before this day. And this day, when he yearned with a mighty passion to destroy his tormentor, he was forced to tell himself that his duty lay in a different path. For what would come to Harrison Mell in case his gun hung for a fraction of a second in the holster and he should fall before the fire of Jarvis?

He saw men pass him with strange, eager looks. They were all hurrying downtown. They had all heard of the challenge, therefore, and they were gathering to see the two ruffians in battle.

But he went homeward with the same unhurried, irregular step, fighting back the impulse that raged stronger and stronger in his breast. While he cooked the supper, he knew that the crowd was still thickening in the center of the village; he could see the big form of Jarvis stalking back and forth, enjoying the center of the stage, and resting his long hands upon his hips. He could hear the whispers of expectation running from lip to lip. He could see the faces of the women, watching, frightened, from behind the adjacent windows. But he went grimly on with the kitchen work.

After all, this was the most cruel of all tortures. To be called an unnatural brute was one thing; to be called a rank coward was quite another. And he had to say aloud to himself, over and over: "All that matters now is Dad."

Someone came hurrying with light steps up to the front door. He went to the door and saw Sue in the act of entering, but when she saw him, she paused, very pale and frightened. "I thought that you . . . I thought . . . ," she breathed, and then she whipped out through the door again and was gone.

She, too, had heard then. She, too, would despise him for having failed to appear on the battlefield. But when he thought of this, there was another picture of a more potent power and that was of Harrison Mell being stunned, one arm fallen across the seat of the chair, and his head lopped over on the loose shoulder. That picture kept him patiently in the house, and that picture, flying between his eyes and the print, made him read the news as he sat at the bedside of Harrison Mell this evening.

Later he heard a wrangle of voices outside the house, calling insults. That must be Jarvis and his crew, he knew. He merely rose to close the window and keep the sounds from the ears of his father. Then he went back to his chair and resumed the reading from the daily *Journal*. Nothing could be missed. The great problem of the protective tariff was being discussed by two powerfully wordy debaters, and he must read every word, while his father lay in silence and blinked thoughtfully as each of the debaters made his points.

When he went to bed, Snoozer was reasonably sure that he could not sleep, but sleep was merciful, after all, and came in a sudden black wave to envelop him, for the first time in forty-eight hours. And when he wakened, the sun was already high, streaming through his window, while a million motes danced in its rays. He had barely time to cook breakfast, bring it to his father, and then hurry away to reach the blacksmith shop by eight o'clock.

While he was still two blocks away, he could see what was waiting for him.

The whole population of Wooster seemed to be lingering in the neighborhood of the blacksmith shop. They were loitering in groups here and there. They were thick about the doors of the smithy itself. They were crowded upon the steps of the Dunton house across the street, and women were packed thick behind the Dunton windows in the first and second stories. They had come again to see the show of which they had been disappointed last night.

Where was the sheriff now? Gone about his business like a

wise man that knew that no matter who fell in this combat, whether one or both, the law gained by the destruction of rascals. After the guns had stopped barking, he would appear in due time and gather in the wounded for the jail.

They sighted Snoozer in the distance, and there was a white flashing in the crowd as all faces turned toward him. So Snoozer went on slowly. Once, instinctively, he reached for his revolver and gripped the butt like a friend's hand. But he drew his fingers away suddenly.

Old man Hanson, the Swede, came hurrying past him, coming away from the clusters near the smithy. He paused and clutched at the shoulder of Snoozer.

"Snoozer," he said, "go back home. It ain't right. Not for him to murder you nor for you to murder him. Get back home, Snoozer."

But Snoozer struck the detaining hand away, and went on. Retreat could not save him. It was merely to delay the agony that must come, sooner or later.

He passed through the outer circles. He spoke pleasantly to those around him, and they answered him in the absent-minded fashion, watching him with a sort of curious horror, as though they could not cast their eyes enough upon the picture of a man who was about to be slain.

In thirty seconds a red chapter of Wooster's history would be written.

He passed through the inner circle, and there was Jarvis, standing tall and thin, before the door of the shop, Jarvis the impeccable of dress, with three or four of his ruffians standing to the side, like jackals following the lion.

Snoozer walked straight on, and a little gasp went up from the crowd. Somewhere in the distance there was a shrill, small sound. Perhaps a woman had screamed inside the Dunton house. Snoozer could not tell. For, with all his soul, he was staring into the eyes of Jarvis and yearning to twitch out his revolver.

Then Jarvis snarled like the beast that he was, and into his hand flashed the length of the Colt revolver. Snoozer, although he halted, merely dropped his hands to his sides. He saw Jarvis lurch and stagger a bit forward as he released his finger from the trigger, so set had he been to fire and so great had been the effort to relax his grip.

There was another breath of amazement from the onlookers, and upon the face of Jarvis a dawning expression of bewilderment and then unutterable loathing and scorn. He walked straight up to Snoozer, his gun covering his enemy.

"I thought it was a man," said Jarvis. "It ain't. It's a rat!"

And he struck Snoozer across the mouth with his open hand. A red mist passed before the eyes of Snoozer Mell. But, the shock having tumbled the hat from his head, Snoozer merely leaned and picked it up and settled it again. Then he looked back into the eyes of Jarvis.

Whatever Jarvis saw, it was something that made him change color, and he gave back a little snarling deep in his throat, flicking his glance up and down the body of Snoozer as though he were choosing a place for his bullet. But Snoozer went on again, and through the door of the shop, and took off his coat and hung it up in the little office. Coming out of the office, he picked up his fourteen-pound sledge.

"What's the first thing this mornin'?" Snoozer said with still lips.

So stunned were the beholders that it was not until that moment that they recovered enough even to speak, and then their voices sounded in the ear of Snoozer like a deep groan, formless, without words, saving for one phrase from someone standing nearby. "He's taken water. A yellow Chinaman could lick him now."

Although his back was toward the crowd, Snoozer could guess that they were melting away behind him, slowly, in clusters, saying nothing as they departed.

Then someone said: "Mister Jarvis, if I was you, I'd be gettin' out of Wooster."

"I'll take my time," said Jarvis.

"You ain't got no time in this town!" answered the stern voice, and others joined in the muttering. For it seemed that Snoozer, in his fall, had stung the pride of all Wooster. In his shame, he had shamed every citizen. And Jarvis, having surveyed those threatening faces, found that discretion was much the better part of too much valor. He took the good advice and left Wooster, never to return.

Then Snoozer saw old Loomis, going toward the forge where he began to work the bellows, slowly, rather leaning upon it trying to work up the dying fire among the coals. When he turned a little, Snoozer had sight of a white, sick face.

How great, indeed, had been his fall.

XII

"HAPPY NEWS"

At least there was white glowing iron on the anvil before him, and some of his grief and his self-horror could be put into the swinging of the fourteen-pound sledge. He made it play around his head like a feather, and the force of his blows smashed the hot iron out of shape, but Loomis said nothing. He merely continued to tap with his guiding hammer, and let the wrecking shower fall where it would. He put the iron back in the coals and once more began to ply the handle of the bellows while Snoozer stepped back among the shadows.

It would not do. Work could not save him. The horror of

188

that morning would stay with him the rest of his life and waken him in the cold middle of the night, gasping and weak. Minutes passed. He looked up, at last, wondering why Loomis was not ready for the sledge again, and then he saw that the grim old man had forgotten to work the bellows, and merely stood beside it resting his fingers on the handle, fallen into a profound muse.

A shadow ran across the doorway. He looked up to see the face of Sue, pale and with reddened eyes, and she came straight to him with her hands clasped together.

"I've heard about it all. I've heard about everything that's happened," she said. "Oh, Alfred, what a great, noble thing you've done!"

"Me?" Snoozer said, reeling to his feet and looking down to her. "Me?"

Old Loomis gaped at them from the distant shadows in the rear of the shop, while the fire died in the forge.

"You, you!" said the girl. "No one realizes just now. They don't understand that it was for Uncle Harrison that you . . . that you . . . oh, poor boy!" She choked and drew a great breath. "It's about Uncle Harrison that I've come. You must go back home at once. Doctor Bostwick. . . ."

"Dad is dying," Snoozer stated heavily. "I knew it would be no good."

"No, no. I mean . . . I can't tell you. Doctor Bostwick. . . ."

He followed her into the blazing sun of the street and there was the good doctor, hurrying and pointing toward them.

"You go ahead, Sue," he gasped out to the girl. "Let me have a chance to talk to Snoozer. Lord God, who would have thought that it would turn out this way? Who would have thought it?"

He gathered the arm of Snoozer within his own and began to lead him carefully along. One would have thought that

Snoozer was a weak old man or a blind cow, to see the cautious, gentle manner of the doctor.

"Look here," Snoozer insisted. "I ain't got a right to be handled like a child. You tell me the facts. I'll stand 'em. It was my dad. If Dad is dyin' . . . or if he's dead . . . I'll stand it. You just tell me now."

"My Lord," said the doctor, "how am I going to begin?"

"Say yes or no. That's enough."

"It was all a mistake. About you, Snoozer. Wait a minute . . . how the devil am I to put it?"

Snoozer waited. Something in his brain was numb, and he was trying to fumble his way toward an understanding of the miracle that people were beginning to change toward him. The doctor had changed. Sue had changed. There she was, running on ahead in haste. Perhaps to get more quickly to her Uncle Harrison. But what had this to do with their gentleness toward him? If his father was dying as a result of the blow that he, Snoozer, had struck?

"The other night," said the doctor, talking in a voice that was half a grunt, "I had a hurry call from your father. When I went to him, he was sitting in the dining room."

"Sitting?" Snoozer cried.

"Yes."

"I see. He busted down later on. Go on."

"Your father told me what happened."

Snoozer winced.

"And he told me that he knew he had seen you for the last time, because he said that he was certain that you would always be ashamed to face him again. And he told me, Snoozer, that it was breaking his heart. He told me that if ever a man had an excuse for striking his father, he had given you that excuse, because he had gone and . . . something about Sue, I think . . . dear girl."

"Leave that," muttered Snoozer.

"He said that he had to bring you back, and that he had thought of a plan for it. He would pretend that you had seriously disabled him . . . almost permanently. Do you see?"

Snoozer stopped short and dragged off his hat and let the burning sun fall upon his head and upon his face.

"You'll never forgive him . . . or me, Snoozer. Because it was I who suggested the paralytic stroke. But I thought . . . and he thought, lad, that you were far gone, and that some decisive thing had to be done to try to redeem you. For my part, freely, I was in doubt and told him to wash his hands of you. But he told me that there was gold in your heart. That there could not help but be good in you because you were your mother's son."

"Did he say that?" whispered Snoozer.

"Aye, Snoozer, he said that. He loves you, boy, in his own, silent way. And a silent love is better and greater than a noisy one. You understand what I mean? He would have done for you, if he had had a chance, a thing just as great and as fine, I think, as this wonderful thing you've done for him this morning. Oh, Snoozer, lad, before the day is an hour older, people will begin to understand what it is that you have done. And then. . . ."

Snoozer began to hurry down the street with his swift, noiseless step. The doctor hurried and pattered along beside him.

"Before you go into the house . . . tell me that you'll forgive him, Snoozer?"

Snoozer said not a word, but walked on faster, and the same stunned, awakening look was on his face.

The doctor fell into an agony of apprehension. "Your father is frantic, boy. He's dressing, and groaning, and cursing himself and me. He's heard about you and . . . the

191

dog, Jarvis. He's heard about how you took your shame. Snoozer, tell me that, when you meet him, you'll forgive him freely."

Still, Snoozer said not a word, but began to hurry so that he was almost running, and the poor doctor was forced to exert himself so much to keep up that he was gasping and panting at the side of the youth, and could not put his words together in sensible fashion.

Through the gate and into the house ran Snoozer, and, casting open the front door, he almost ran against poor Sue, who stretched out her arms to block his way. "Alfred! Alfred . . . you aren't angry with Uncle Harrison?"

Snoozer lifted her gently from his way.

"Where is he?" he asked with a sort of hungry eagerness, and, turning into the living room, there he saw the big form of Harrison Mell, and the great ugly head, and the eyes filled with unspeakable concern.

Snoozer ran straight to him and caught him in his arms like a child. Behind him he heard the happy call of Sue, and then her sobbing.

"Snoozer," stammered the blacksmith, "it was a low-down trick that I played on you. But, oh, boy, I didn't know the manner of man that you were. Will you forgive me?"

Snoozer took a step back and held his father by the points of those Herculean shoulders. "Dad," he said, "I've been through hell, but I'd go through it again to have you on your feet like this! What's happened don't count, if you and me can be friends."

"Lad, lad," said the blacksmith in a broken voice, "if ghosts walk the earth, there's one in this room with a happy heart. But yonder is poor Sue, crying her eyes out and the doctor can't stop her. Nor I. Snoozer, wouldn't you try your luck?"

Snoozer obeyed. When the doctor arrived, Snoozer took Sue out into the garden where the bright flower faces were stirring in the sunshine and the green leaves were glistening and dripping with the yellow light. And all at once Sue was no longer crying.

"I dunno what made you cry," Snoozer said as gently as he could.

"Happiness!" Sue answered.

"Ah," Snoozer said sadly, "it's Steve, then?"

"Steve?" cried the girl fiercely. "I . . . I despise him. He went to *watch* you this morning. I'll never face him again, and I've told him so. I'd rather have you . . . oh, Snoozer, what have I said?"

The answer of Snoozer was witnessed by the doctor as he came out at the front door, and he retreated so suddenly that his heel caught and he rolled back into the house like a ball.

About the Author

Max Brand is the best-known pen name of Frederick Faust, creator of Dr. Kildare, Destry, and many other fictional characters popular with readers and viewers worldwide. Faust wrote for a variety of audiences in many genres. His enormous output, totaling approximately thirty million words or the equivalent of 530 ordinary books, covered nearly every field: crime, fantasy, historical romance, espionage, Westerns, science fiction, adventure, animal stories, love, war, and fashionable society, big business and big medicine. Eighty motion pictures have been based on his work along with many radio and television programs. For good measure he also published four volumes of poetry. Perhaps no other author has reached more people in more different ways.

Born in Seattle in 1892, orphaned early, Faust grew up in the rural San Joaquin Valley of California. At Berkeley he became a student rebel and one-man literary movement, contributing prodigiously to all campus publications. Denied a degree because of unconventional conduct, he embarked on a series of adventures culminating in New York City where, after a period of near starvation, he received simultaneous recognition as a serious poet and successful author of fiction. Later, he traveled widely, making his home in New York, then in Florence, and finally in Los Angeles.

Once the United States entered the Second World War,

Faust abandoned his lucrative writing career and his work as a screenwriter to serve as a war correspondent with the infantry in Italy, despite his fifty-one years and a bad heart. He was killed during a night attack on a hilltop village held by the German army. New books based on magazine serials or unpublished manuscripts or restored versions continue to appear so that, alive or dead, he has averaged a new book every four months for seventy-five years. Beyond this, some work by him is newly reprinted every week of every year in one or another format somewhere in the world. A great deal more about this author and his work can be found in *The Max Brand Companion* (Greenwood Press, 1997) edited by Jon Tuska and Vicki Piekarski. His next **Five Star Western** will be *The Tyrant of Guarpamal.*